CW01112676

WHAT WE DID ON OUR HOLIDAYS

By the same author:

STREET SLEEPER
THE KNOT GARDEN

WHAT WE DID ON OUR HOLIDAYS

Geoff Nicholson

Hodder & Stoughton
LONDON SYDNEY AUCKLAND TORONTO

British Library Cataloguing in Publication Data
Nicholson, Geoff, 1953–
  What we did on our holidays.
  I. Title
  823'.914[F]

ISBN 0-340-51362-4

Copyright © 1990 by Geoff Nicholson

First published in Great Britain 1990

All rights reserved. No part of this publication may be
reproduced or transmitted in any form or by any means,
electronic or mechanical, including photocopying,
recording, or any information storage and retrieval system,
without either prior permission in writing from the
publisher or a licence permitting restricted copying.
In the United Kingdom such licences are issued by the
Copyright Licensing Agency, 33–34 Alfred Place, London WC1E 7DP.

Published by Hodder and Stoughton,
a division of Hodder and Stoughton Ltd,
Mill Road, Dunton Green, Sevenoaks, Kent TN13 2YA
Editorial Office: 47 Bedford Square, London WC1B 3DP

Typeset by Hewer Text Composition Services, Edinburgh
Printed in Great Britain by St Edmundsbury Press Ltd, Bury St Edmunds, Suffolk

WHAT WE DID ON OUR HOLIDAYS

Prologue

I suppose it all started as I was enjoying a bottled lager in the saloon-bar of the Devonshire Arms with one or two chaps from work. I was celebrating, though 'celebrating' probably isn't the right word, my forty-fifth birthday. I was leaning on the bar, minding my own business, talking to Terry about his chances of promotion (slim I had to admit) when I experienced what can only be described as an intense bout of middle-aged angst. The lager turned to ashes in my mouth, my eyes, people told me later, glazed over, and searing doubts and uncertainties crowded in on me like so many gawpers at a road accident.

I wasn't very good company for the rest of the evening. I kept asking myself some pretty tricky questions. Who was I? Where was I going? Who were my fellow-travellers? Did I know myself? Did I know my own wife? My children? Did they know me? Was there perhaps more to life than working in the bought ledger office of a major chain of furniture retailers?

I couldn't come up with any answers then. In fact the more questions I asked the less I knew. The time had come to take stock. I looked unflinchingly at myself in the etched mirror on the wall of the Devonshire Arms, and I'm not afraid to say that I didn't entirely like what I saw.

Days passed. My brain was in a turmoil. I'll sound like a silly so-and-so if I say I was gripped by the urge to make my life more profound and meaningful, but, silly or not, that's exactly the urge I *was* gripped by.

I wanted to get off this rat race of a roundabout for a while, take time to think things through, to tarry a while, to look and listen, to sniff the roses, to get to know myself and my loved ones that little bit better. What I needed, I realised, was a holiday.

For a while I'd been thinking that one way or another this year's holiday ought to be a little bit special. It's probably the last one the four of us will take as a family. The kids are growing up fast and I realise that they find their old Dad's pace a little pedestrian. Next year my boy Max will probably be away at a poly studying earth sciences (God and a lenient examiner willing), while my lovely daughter Sally has said she wants to go on a French exchange, preferably to Lourdes. Even my trim and attractive wife Kathleen has suggested that next year we take separate 'singles' holidays. I'm not the sort of man to stand in my family's way. I realise that the pattern of family life must change over the years, however, I thought that was all the more reason why they should indulge me, and do it my way this one last time.

They weren't immediately agreeable. They all had their own ideas about what makes a holiday special. A fortnight in Serengeti, a retreat to a Tibetan monastery, and a tour of the flesh-pots of Bangkok were all mooted; and while I lent a sympathetic ear to their suggestions, I have a persuasive tongue and I eventually got them to agree with me. I also had to throw the odd temper tantrum, but it was worth it.

It's long seemed to me that there's only one recipe for guaranteed vacation success, and that is, in a word, caravanning.

Better safe than sorry has always been my motto, and I didn't want to take any chances on this epochal holiday, so I thought we should choose a place that we know and love. Such a place is the Tralee Carapark and Holiday Centre, Skegness.

It is a well-designed, attractively appointed, carefully screened, compact site, on level ground, with trees and bushes, sloping gently towards the sea on one side, with small but sylvan hills to the rear. It has outstanding panoramic views and is genuinely picturesque. There are extensive showering and toilet facilities, a site shop, a launderette, a children's playground, and Calor gas supply.

I'm pleased to say that it's free from TV lounges, cafés, games rooms, licensed bars, swimming-pools, cinemas, stables, hairdressing salons, communal barbecue areas and artificial ski-slopes. Motorcycles are not welcome.

All right, I admit that the term 'Holiday Centre' may be a slight exaggeration, considering how little is actually on offer, but as I told Max and Sally when they tried to talk me into a trek through the Sahara, I know what we like.

Children are a joy but they're also a worry. You want to do your best for them but in the end there's not so very much that you *can* do. You offer helpful fatherly advice but they've got to be free to make their own mistakes.

My boy Max, for instance, isn't exactly the son every father wishes for. He's a bit moody and a bit laddish, always a bad combination. He's very fond of animals and watching nature programmes on television, and you'd think that ought to be a civilising influence; but he has shocking table manners, and when he loses his temper, which he does all too often for my liking, he tends to smash to pieces anything that comes to hand. He means well but he's not as thoughtful and sensitive as I'd like a son of mine to be.

By contrast, my lovely daughter Sally is, if anything, too sensitive by half. If she's not pressing flowers or reading poetry she's writing her own hymns and praying for world peace. Still, it's probably just a fad that most girls go through. She'll no doubt turn out as normal as the rest of us, and I'm sure she'll soon give up her ambition to be a nun.

Anyway, no doubt there'll be more about Max and Sally later, and about Kathleen and myself, and about life and love and death, and most of the other big issues.

In order to clarify my thoughts and feelings, and help me get to know myself and my loved ones better, I've decided to keep a diary of the holiday. I went into my local newsagent and demanded their finest hardback, narrow-ruled exercise-book.

I admit it crossed my mind to use a slightly more high-tech form of journal. I might have hired a video camera and filmed the holiday, but I'm not very good with technology and focus would have been a problem. It crossed my mind that I might get a tape recorder and talk into it every night before turning in, but that wouldn't have suited me either. Unlike so many people, I'm not deeply in love with the sound of my own voice.

So I'll be using the old-fashioned written word. Call me a

Luddite if you like. It was good enough for Pepys so it's good enough for me. Of course Pepys did have certain advantages that I don't. He had fairly gripping subject matter in the Plague and the Fire of London, whereas I have two weeks in a caravan park.

Some might think that I'm in the wrong place and don't have time enough to explore the heights and depths of being, but I'm a man of modest ambition, and I feel sure that I'll have enough scope to record some lively outer events, some innermost thoughts, and (who knows) maybe even the odd revelation.

Saturday

Well, we've arrived.

The drive here, I need hardly say, was a complete nightmare. The motor was newly polished and serviced, oil and tyre pressure checked, full of petrol and raring to go.

If I'd only had myself, my car and my own driving to worry about all would have been fine. Unfortunately when you're at the wheel of your car you have every other damn fool on the road to worry about as well. Some drivers baffle me, they really do. Where's the courtesy, the lane discipline, the obedience of speed limits? Do they know their stopping distances? Do they signal correctly and in good time? Do they ask themselves before attempting a manoeuvre, is it safe? Is it convenient? Is it lawful? Do they *heck*?

Quite simply I ran into the back of some damn fool who braked, completely without warning, to avoid knocking down some old crone with a walking-frame who'd wandered into the middle of a zebra crossing.

I think I'm as caring and humane as the next person, but, as I contemplated the damage done to the front of my car, I couldn't see that the world would have been much worse off for the loss of one elderly dodderer.

The driver of the car I'd run into leapt from his seat, hopping mad, and looking as though he intended to do me violence. However, he took a good look at the back of his car, which appeared entirely unblemished, looked at my car, which was blemished good and proper, and let out a gale of scarcely controlled mirth.

'You're a very lucky man,' he said.

'I'm afraid I don't quite see that,' I replied.

'Very lucky indeed. If you'd damaged my car I'd have damaged your face. Permanently.'

Until this moment I'd been in a pretty sunny sort of mood, but this chap was threatening to dampen my spirits. Luckily he returned to his vehicle and drove off, taking various bits of my headlamps with him.

As I cleared up the remaining broken bits of my car, I reflected how prudent it was of me to take out fully comprehensive insurance. I suppose it could all have been a lot worse. It wasn't the start to the holiday that I'd have chosen but at least nobody got hurt and the car was still driveable.

My boy Max tried to cheer me up by saying that if he (the other driver) had laid so much as a finger on me, then he (Max) would have beaten him to an unpleasant pulp. I thanked Max. It's funny how a crisis can bring a family together.

The rest of the journey was pleasantly uneventful. Slow, tiring, and fraught with danger because of the remarkable crassness of other road users, but uneventful.

We did a little community singing, at least *I* did. The rest of the family wouldn't join in, so it became something of a solo recital. I treated them to more or less my complete repertoire, from 'These Foolish Things' to 'Scarlet Ribbons' via a whole range of well-known crowd-pleasers. It certainly made the journey go with a swing so far as *I* was concerned.

And so to the Tralee Carapark and Holiday Centre, where all sorts of earlier holiday memories came flooding back. It isn't exactly as I remembered it. They've built a burger bar, a pool hall and a crazy golf course, which are far from welcome additions as far as I'm concerned; but I hope the spirit of the place remains intact. There also seems to be an unacceptable amount of litter strewn all over the place: burger wrappers and used condoms to name but two items. I'm doing my best to ignore them. Perhaps I can organise a litter patrol later in the week.

Went to our caravan. There's a sign on the inside of the door which reads, 'Please leave this caravan in the state you would wish to find it.' It appears that the previous occupants would like to find a caravan full of stale crumbs (not that fresh crumbs would be any more welcome), handfuls of hair, used tea-bags, cheesy milk bottles, scum and grease in the sink, and a devastatingly foul smell coming from the chemical toilet.

'Never mind,' I said brightly. 'We can have this place spick and span in next to no time if we all pitch in.'

However, the others didn't pitch in, so it took me a very considerable amount of time. Still, I whistled while I worked, and I got that caravan looking like a palace. It was a slightly cramped, pokey and evil-smelling palace, but a palace all the same.

It took a while to solve the problem of the chemical toilet but eventually I discovered that someone had unceremoniously dropped a dead cat down the pan. I thought that was pretty unnecessary. I fished the corpse out and deposited it in a bin by the burger bar. It was a dirty job but somebody had to do it, and I knew there wasn't much chance of that somebody being Kathleen, Sally or Max.

The lock on the caravan door didn't seem to work properly either, so as a last finishing touch I rigged up a couple of nails and a bit of string to hold it shut.

'Very inventive,' Kathleen said on her return.

It's funny she should say that because I've often thought that I'd like to invent something. It could be something really simple yet something that everybody needs, like the safety-pin, or central heating, or mayonnaise. Not that I eat a lot of mayonnaise. Call me an old eccentric but I've always had a bit of a thing about other people's food. If I were to go out and buy an egg-mayonnaise sandwich, say, from some cheap and cheerful sandwich bar, I couldn't eat and enjoy it. I'd be forever worrying that somebody might have spat in the egg mixture.

If I ever ate out in restaurants or, God help us, at burger bars, I'd be constantly inspecting the food, on the look-out for snot, phlegm, hairs, toe-nail clippings, ear-wax etc. etc. These days you might come across something worse than any of those, especially in mayonnaise.

So, in consequence, we don't eat out. We favour self-catering; hearty, uncontaminated cooking prepared by my wife's loving fingers. Much more economical too!

Also, as a matter of fact, there are few restaurants in the land that can serve up such mouth-watering morsels as Kathleen. She's always a first-rate cook, but on holiday she really does pull out all the stops. I know that in the next fortnight I'll have all sorts of tempting treats to look forward to. Just the thought of her beetroot and liver supreme sets my saliva racing.

While she was rustling up a taste sensation this evening I thought I'd be neighbourly and go and introduce myself to the folk in the adjacent caravan.

They seem nice enough young people. They're foreign but not offensively so, and their name is Garcia: Axel and Iris.

I knocked on the caravan door. A man's lightly Hispanic voice invited me in. The owner of the voice, the husband, was a swarthy, perspiring, unshaven type. He was smoking a cheroot, wearing a poncho, and he was hawking at intervals into a brass spitoon. He sat with his cowboy boots on the table and whittled a stick with a mean-looking knife.

He seemed a little the worse for alcohol and was very insistent that I joined him for a pre-prandial tipple. I said I'd be delighted to accept a small gin and tonic or a bottled lager, but he found that rather risible, and, despite my protests, he forced me to swig from a bottle of tequila. I suppose it wasn't too bad if you like that sort of thing, unfortunately I don't, and consequently I had considerable trouble keeping it down. He didn't help matters any by slapping me hard on the back and calling me gringo.

His wife, not an unappealing woman, though perhaps a little too buxom, raven-tressed, flashing-eyed and sultry for my tastes, offered me what I believe are called Tex-Mex *hors d'oeuvres*; small, alarming concoctions with chili, garlic (one of my pet hates), avocado and refried beans. Fortunately I was able to decline, saying they'd spoil my meal (and I'm sure they would have).

Throughout my visit a record of 'Spanish Eyes' was playing at quite an unnecessary volume, and every so often Axel would clap his hands violently while Iris would perform a few passionate flamenco steps. Not, I'd have thought, the sort of thing you do when you have a neighbour round.

I was happy to get back to my own caravan. Nevertheless, I'm a tolerant man, I take as I find, and I'm sure that, given willingness on both sides, we can become fast friends with the Garcias.

After Kathleen's delicious meal, in the course of which, alas, I had to pull Max up for his poor table manners, we were all a bit tuckered out. But I still managed to persuade the family to play a nice game of pontoon. I know pontoon can be fairly exciting and tiring in itself so I suppose we were fortunate that the run of the cards was low-key and easy on the nerves.

However, our nerves were set rudely ajangle when, quite out of the blue, a house-brick was tossed through our caravan window. There was a note attached to the brick that read, 'Go back where you belong. Death to the Evil Empire'. It was unsigned.

Well, I was shocked. That sort of thing could seriously sour the holiday atmosphere, but I was determined not to let it.

'Probably the brick was thrown in a spirit of misplaced holiday exuberance,' I said.

'Probably just kids,' Kathleen agreed.

We returned to our game of pontoon, but I have to admit I was a bit rattled. The throwing of bricks wasn't a customary occurrence in the Tralee Carapark and Holiday Centre that I used to know and love. My concentration must have been shattered because I immediately lost the bank and before very long I'd been completely cleaned out of matches. I took it like a good loser.

It's late now, well past midnight. The family have turned in and are sleeping the sleep of the just. I'm sitting here, burning the midnight bulb, tired yet eager to reflect on the day and its events, and to jot it all down in my journal.

I suppose it hasn't been an absolutely perfect start to a holiday. A car crash, a filthy caravan and a smashed window wouldn't be on most people's ideal itinerary, but at least we're here. Life and limb are perfectly intact. Now all we have to do is relax and enjoy ourselves.

I've always had a bit of a philosophical streak in me, and as I sit here writing these words I keep thinking about free will and predestination. Here we are with a whole fortnight ahead of us and I can't help wondering what sort of time we're going to have. Will it be the holiday of a lifetime, or will it be rainy, miserable and not much fun at all?

And the thing I really want to know is, is it all determined in advance? Has somebody or something already decided what sort of time we're going to have, so that all we're doing is going through the motions? Or are we masters of our own fate? Are we free to make our holiday exactly what we want it to be?

This is the sort of thing they don't put in the brochures. It's a rum old world isn't it? Kathleen has just rolled over in her sleep and murmured, 'Come on Eric. Come to bed. Let's make babies.' That's a turn of events that I for one couldn't have predicted. Just as well my name's Eric, eh? Ah well, I can't deny that woman anything.

And so to bed.

Sunday

Woke very early. I didn't get a very good night's sleep. I had some fairly vivid dreams; that I was still at work, that I had to enter a whole quarter's transactions in the bought ledger, that I had to do it all by myself before I could go home, that some invoices had gone missing, that I didn't have a pen that worked, that the entries were written in some sort of code, that the auditors had found all sorts of terrible errors that were my responsibility; that sort of thing. I was glad to wake up.

I wasn't as glad as all that because I immediately detected that I was developing the symptoms of a summer cold. It's been said, generally by members of my own family, that I'm something of a hypochondriac. This is untrue. It's true that I tend to shove down quite a lot of medicines, but that's only because I get a lot of ill health.

Yesterday, for example, on the way here, I was suffering quite badly from a headache and car-sickness. Long, arduous journeys have that effect on me. I didn't complain at the time, and I'm not really complaining now, I just think it's the sort of thing that ought to go in a journal.

Today the headache and car-sickness are gone but I have a stuffed-up feeling, a sore throat and the beginnings of a blocked sinus. But I'm not a man to go on about his own sufferings, and I certainly won't let a little thing like illness spoil my holiday.

Discovered over breakfast that I don't have fully comprehensive motor insurance. In fact I don't have any motor insurance at all. I suppose it's my own fault. I've always left the paying of bills to Kathleen, and it appears she failed to renew our insurance policy. I can't really blame her for it. She says she thought it was a terrible waste of money since I'm such a safe and careful driver and I've gone all these years without so much as a scrape. The one thing that does puzzle me though, is that I quite clearly remember giving her the money to pay the premium.

'What happened to that money?' I asked.

'What do you think happened to it? Do you think I used it to buy silk shirts for my fancy man?' she joked.

I tried to manage a smile, but I admit it didn't come easily. Some husbands would have 'blown their top' but I didn't. I'm pleased to say that's never been my style. There's no use crying over spilt milk, is there? I also didn't want mundane commercial considerations to spoil my relationship with Kathleen. I like to think our marriage is based on higher things.

After breakfast I took her aside and asked her if she truly knew herself.

'Yes,' she said without a moment's hesitation.

'And do you truly know me and the kids?'

'Oh yes,' she said just as unhesitatingly.

'And don't you ever think there might be more to life than this?'

'No,' she said. 'This is life and this is all there is to it.'

'I wish I had your confidence.'

'So do I.'

We sat there for quite a while and didn't say anything. There was no need to. We understood each other.

'You know what else?'

'No,' I said.

'I'd really like to be shafted from behind by an Arab with a big tool, who really knows how to use it.'

When possible on holiday I like to go for a morning constitutional. It clears away the cobwebs and helps you see the world afresh. This morning I hadn't gone very far before I fell in step with a personable young chap who was also staying at the Tralee. He was very clean and tidy and I must say I liked the cut of his jib. However, he did have a bit of a haunted look about him, and the reason for this became clear as the conversation progressed or rather failed to progress because the poor chap had rather a stutter. Personally I didn't think it was so very bad as stutters go, but the young chap seemed to think it had completely ruined his life.

He said, 'If it wasn't f-f-for this stutter I could have had a career doing v-voice-overs for television commercials.'

I pride myself on being able to see the other chap's point of view but I felt bound to say that in my opinion he hadn't really thought this one through.

'Look at *me*,' I said. 'I don't have a stutter, do I? Yet you don't see me doing voice-overs. There are millions of people in Britain without stutters but they're hardly all walking into jobs doing voice-overs, are they?'

'That's easy f-for you to say.'

'It's like saying if only you were an idle good-for-nothing, you could be a plumber. All plumbers are idle good-for-nothings, but not all idle good-for-nothings are plumbers. I'm sure getting to do voice-overs depends on who you know, which university you went to, and who you drink with, not just on not having a stutter.'

This didn't seem to cheer him up very much.

'Do you think B-B-Burt Reynolds would be where he is today if he stuttered?' he asked. 'Or B-B-Bryan F-F-F-Forbes? Or B-B-Beryl B-B-B-B-Bainbridge?'

'Probably not,' I admitted. 'But I'm sure you've got other qualities that they *don't* have.'

'All I've got's a stutter.'

'You just have to do what you can with what you've got,' I said, perhaps a bit lamely.

'You could be right,' he said. 'I'm probably just deceiving myself about v-voice-overs. I should aim lower. Maybe I could b-b-be a b-b-b-bingo caller.'

I didn't have the heart to tell him he was barmy. Maybe he wasn't. If you don't have hopes and dreams when you're young then I don't suppose you ever will. On the other hand I do think it pays to have realistic hopes and dreams. We said goodbye and I went on my way thinking about the nature of youth.

It's a funny thing in my opinion, youth. Sometimes I look at young people and I can't deny that I feel a bit envious. They're good-looking and healthy and rich and sexy; and I think yes, I wish I were like that instead of middle-aged and ordinary. Then

I think back to when I was young, and the truth is I wasn't good-looking and healthy and rich and sexy then any more than I am now. And if I were young today I probably still wouldn't be all those things. I'd just be young and ordinary, and I'd be worried about the future, and about getting a girlfriend, and about spots and pimples. So sometimes it seems to me that I'm not too badly off being middle-aged and ordinary.

Take my lovely daughter Sally. We were washing up after lunch and I was trying, very casually, to get to know her better.

'Don't you ever wonder what it's all about, Sally?' I asked.

'No,' she replied.

'Well perhaps I didn't wonder about the big issues when I was your age either.'

'I've no need to wonder,' she said, 'because I'm absolutely certain in my perceptions of the divine purpose.'

'Well, that's one way of looking at it.'

'No,' she said. (And I detected that she was getting a bit high and mighty now.) 'There's only one way of looking at it, and I know the way. God's way.'

The truth is I've never known where I stand on religion. I suppose I don't stand anywhere. I suppose I move uneasily from foot to foot. I'm sure religion's a good thing just so long as people don't get carried away with it.

'Why don't we both get down on our knees here and now,' Sally said, 'and let's pray together.'

I told her not to be so damn silly. I also told her she wasn't too old to get her legs slapped. She got a martyred look on her face and threw down the tea-towel.

'There's still plenty of drying up to be done young lady,' I said.

Sally was almost out of the caravan by then but as she got to the door she turned and retorted. 'Excuse me. I must be about my Father's business.'

'Going off to do a bit of bought ledger, are you?' I rejoindered, but she'd gone by then. Ah youth!

It appears there must be an airfield nearby. It was mid-afternoon and the sun was big and yellow and suddenly I heard the sound of an aeroplane engine. It was an old World War One sort of noise and before long I saw the plane itself, a Sopwith Camel if I wasn't mistaken. It banked out of the sun and flew exceptionally low, low enough for me to see the pilot. I gave him a cheery wave and he gave a thumbs-down signal. I don't know what that meant but I was then treated to an absolutely spectacular exhibition of stunt flying.

The machine climbed steeply in the sky. The pilot throttled back, attempted a stall turn. The craft shoved its nose down and fell like a stone. It went into a spin and looked sure to crash but, seconds before it would have hit the ground, the engine sparked back to life and the plane ascended again, now leaving clouds of black smoke in its slipstream. The pilot headed for the open sea, clipping a few trees as he went. It all looked terribly risky and realistic but no doubt it was all part of the show.

Finally the old biplane appeared to plunge into the sea and that was very lifelike too. I imagine it must have been an advertising stunt for some kind of flying circus. If I see tickets on sale anywhere I'll be the first to snap them up. I've always been a bit of a sucker for rip-roaring entertainment. Also, of course, this kind of display has enormous historical value, especially for the young.

How many men can put their hands on their hearts and say they don't have any vices? Not me. Don't get me wrong, I'm not a drunk or a drug addict or an adulterer or anything of that sort at all, but I am a bit of a slave to tobacco. Yes, yes, yes, I know it's expensive and antisocial and bad for my health, but you can't reason with vice.

Kathleen has banned cigarettes from the house because they're dirty and smelly and might give her cancer. She won't let me smoke in the car, won't let me smoke if we go out together, and, even if I'm out in the garden and she's in the house and she sees me light up, she comes running out and knocks the weed from my lips. I suppose she has a point.

But, I ask myself, what is a holiday for if you can't indulge yourself a bit? And why shouldn't a man of my age have a few crafty drags once in a while if that's what he feels he needs in order to become a whole person?

I have hit upon a plan. Since there is only the one chemical toilet in our caravan, I waited until somebody entered then tried the door and said, 'Don't worry about me, I'll use one in the clean and hygienic shower block.' So off I went. I slipped into a cubicle and lit up. It was the nearest thing to heaven I've known in a long time.

Kathleen's never really been one for roughing it. Personally I could be happy rolling out my sleeping-bag on the edge of a forest somewhere and eating cold baked beans out of a tin, but Kathleen does like a few mod cons. She even thinks that going to the Tralee's launderette is a primitive, unbearable hardship. That's why she doesn't do it. That's why I tipped the family's dirty laundry into a bin liner and set off to do it myself.

Frankly, I was slightly vexed to discover that Kathleen hadn't done the laundry before we set off. I've never wanted Kathleen to become a domestic drudge but I must say it seems to me that bringing four suitcases full of dirty clothes on holiday with you isn't the sort of thing that the averagely competent housewife would do.

I went to the site launderette, put the washing into the machine, started it, thought about this and that. Time passed. I'd got to the drying stage when two young people came into the launderette. I don't know if I'm getting old but I wasn't able to tell whether they were boys or girls, or one of each. I hope it was one of each because they kept necking and feeling each other up. I pretended not to notice.

They hadn't got any laundry with them so I suspected they might be up to no good, but I just carried on with my drying. They asked me to change a pound and I'm one of those fortunate people who always has a lot of change so I was able to oblige, but I was blessed if I could see what they were going to dry.

Well, they opened the door of the big tumble-drier. One of them got in and the other closed the door, put money in the slot, and the drum started to go round. I watched open-mouthed. After a minute or so the one on the outside opened the door, the machine stopped, and they changed places. Another minute and the door was opened, the one inside got out and they started giggling and snogging again.

I felt I really couldn't let this pass without comment.

'What on earth are you doing?' I asked.

'It's a trust game,' one of them said.

'Sorry?' I said.

'You have to trust your partner a lot before you let them lock you in there.'

I could see there was no denying that.

'Isn't it dangerous?'

'Of course it's dangerous. Want to try?'

'No,' I said. 'I can't see my partner going for that. Kathleen, my wife, has been a bit funny so far this holiday but not *that* funny.'

'Not with her, with us.'

'But I hardly know you.'

'That makes it all the more poignant wouldn't you say?'

I mulled it over for a second, then thought what the hell, break the habit of a lifetime and do something wild and zany for once.

'All right,' I said.

I started to get in the drier.

'Only for one minute,' I said. 'Not a second longer.'

'Don't worry. Trust us.'

I did. I had to.

I don't know if you've ever spent a minute in a hot tumble-drier. There are worse things. It's red-hot, airless, you burn your hands on the metal of the drum, you can't breathe very well and you keep being spun round, then falling back to the bottom of the drum and banging your head and getting nauseous. And of course you do get a bit anxious about whether or not you can trust the people who put you in, especially when the people who put you in are two androgynous teenagers you've never seen before.

However, I'm pleased to say that my decision to trust this pair was entirely vindicated. After exactly one minute they opened the door and the drier stopped. Whether it had been a good decision to spend any time at all in the drier is another matter. I came out hardly able to walk, with a blinding headache, and with the urge to throw up. It certainly made me forget my summer cold.

I staggered out of the launderette to get a bit of fresh air and I had a gentle walk round the site to get myself back to rights. Twenty minutes later I went back to the launderette and of course there was no sign of the teenagers. That wasn't so surprising. But incidentally, or perhaps coincidentally, there was no sign of my laundry either.

Kathleen was a bit livid when I got back and told her.

'This would never have happened if we'd gone on a naturist holiday like I suggested,' she said.

There was no denying that either.

Late in the evening I came across my boy Max at the edge of the site. He'd shot a rabbit with some lethal-looking catapult device and now he was skinning it. He seemed to be making a pretty good job of it too.

When he'd finished I took him aside and I said, 'Do you know where you're going to, Max? Do you like the things that life is showing you?'

'Not a lot,' he replied.

Good, I thought, at last I've found something in common with Max.

'Like father, like son,' I said. 'Probably you think there ought to be something more.'

'Too right.'

'And like me you probably have difficulty knowing just what that "something more" should be.'

'Not really.'

'Oh?'

'I want savagery, primitivism, a feeling of being in touch with my animal self.'

'I'm not sure I follow you there, Max old son.'

'I'm talking about atavism, the memory of blood and bone, the knowledge of evil, the inevitability of death.'

I pride myself on being able to see the other chap's point of view, and I really did want to know what Max was on about, especially since he was being unusually chatty for Max, but I suppose you can't teach an old dog new tricks and I was blowed if I could catch his drift.

'We'll talk again about this later,' I said, but I'm not at all sure that we will.

Finally a note on the climate. It seems to me that we've had some freak weather today. It started out fairly inclement with early morning mist and a touch of ground frost. Then it cleared to become cloudy but bright, giving way to sun with scattered showers. Later it became quite a scorcher and the hottest day on record for this time of year. By afternoon it was squally, becoming thunderous with gale force winds. As I write it's a clear night with a chance of snow on higher ground. I must say how pleased I am that we're not on higher ground.

Monday

Had another poor night's sleep. Partly it was bad dreams – of climbing an endless staircase, of losing my shoes, of falling into water – partly it was Kathleen's attentions. I know I shouldn't complain about Kathleen's fondness for me, but it did mean that come seven o'clock this morning I was extremely weary yet I knew I didn't have much chance of getting any more sleep. I decided to get up and go for my constitutional.

I hadn't gone very far before I fell in step with an old gent, also on holiday at the Tralee. He seemed a cheery soul, relaxed, good-humoured and worldly-wise. Our conversation covered a wide range of topics: winter sports, modern architecture, postcard collecting and public transport. He had some lively opinions but nothing particularly extreme until we came to the subject of the younger generation.

'Hanging's not good enough for them,' he said. 'What they need is a spell in the Army.'

I pride myself on being able to see the other chap's point of view so I said, 'You could be right there.'

'Of course I'm right,' he said. 'And if the Army doesn't do the trick they should be flogged and made to perform disgusting sex acts, and have electrodes attached to their genitals and have their feet eaten by red ants.'

'I'm not sure I can go all the way with you on that one,' I said.

He didn't like being disagreed with. His face turned red and his eyes bulged, and he said, 'You'll agree with me or I'll pull your sodding lungs out.'

This presented me with a bit of a problem. I'm the sort of chap who likes to stand up for his beliefs. I hadn't come on holiday to play the hypocrite. On the other hand I hadn't come on holiday to have my lungs pulled out, either. I thought discretion was the better part of valour, and I pride myself on my discretion.

'Oh yes,' I said. 'Now I see your point.'

He was soon his old relaxed, good-humoured, worldly-wise self again. Ah well, it wouldn't do for us all to be alike.

Decided to tackle the problem of getting the car repaired today. I hoped to find some trusty local garage, get them to have a look at it, see what needed doing and put it right in next to no time at a very reasonable cost. Was that asking too much?

For a time it appeared that it was. All up and down the Lincolnshire coast men in blue overalls looked at me, looked at my car, pursed their lips and said there was nothing they could do for me. Sometimes they shook their heads sadly in sympathy. Sometimes they gave a sort of mocking laugh. But, one way or another, they all had too much work on or it was too big or too small a job, or their welder was off sick with his gall-bladder. It was the old story.

Then, when I'd nearly given up all hope, fate finally smiled at me. Life's like that, I find. I came across a garage and used-car emporium called 'Honest Iago's'. It didn't look exactly imposing. The cars for sale looked like overpriced wrecks and they were parked on a rough cinder track. The office was an old garden shed held together by sickly blue paint, and the workshop was built out of old corrugated iron sheets. I was also put off by the fact that the name looked foreign, but beggars can't be choosers and I was desperate enough to give it a try.

A man, Iago I suppose, came out of the workshop. He looked convincingly foreign: Latin looks, sleek hair and a thin mustache, though I know looks aren't everything.

I gave him a cheery 'good day' though I was feeling far from cheery. He didn't respond. He stared at me with big sad eyes. I didn't entirely like the look of him. He walked around my car a few times, scrutinising it closely. He still didn't say a word, though I suppose he did communicate a sort of quiet dignity.

'Well, what do you think?' I asked him when I couldn't stand the silence any longer.

'Fifty quid,' he said.

The voice wasn't noticeably foreign. In fact it was more Rotherham. But whatever accent it had, it was saying what I wanted to hear and quoting a price that was lower than I'd dared to hope for.

'That sounds great,' I said.

'It's a deal then, flower,' he said, reaching into his trouser pocket, producing five oily tenners.

'Eh?' I said. 'What's this?'

'The fifty quid for the car.'

'For my car? I want you to repair it, not buy it!'

'Oh,' he said and then went very quiet again.

I know members of the motor trade aren't known for their towering intellects and their lively conversation but this was ridiculous. He took another silent walking-tour around my car, poked his finger into the radiator, looked closely at the damage. He didn't seem to enjoy looking at my car, but for that matter neither did I in its present condition.

'Is your insurance paying for this?'

'No it isn't!' I said testily.

He looked offended.

'Sorry,' I said. 'I didn't mean to sound testy.'

Another profound silence ensued.

'I suppose we're talking a couple of grand.'

'But the car's barely worth that much,' I protested.

'The car's hardly worth fifty quid,' he muttered under his breath.

I could see I was heading for another disappointment. The only thing to do was to speak to him man to man.

'You look like a reasonable chap,' I began. 'Surely we can come to some sort of arrangement.'

He looked at me blankly.

'Can't we?' I persisted.

'What sort of arrangement, flower?'

'How about I leave the car with you. You give me one of yours as a courtesy car while mine's being fixed. You buckle down to it, pull out all the stops and have the car ready for me in a couple of days, the job well done, showing good craftsmanship and attention to detail, and I'll pay you a hundred pounds. That sort of arrangement.'

It set him thinking. At least he looked as though he was thinking. After a while his face went blank and I couldn't be sure if he was doing anything at all. I didn't want to browbeat the poor chap but I couldn't help thinking that what he really needed was a kick up the backside.

'Is that all right?' I said.

'Yeah, all right.'

I think I must have appealed to his better nature. He set me up with a car from the used lot. It was an old but quite soulful Wartburg. They don't make them like that anymore. The steering was a bit loose and I did end up on the pavement once or twice on the way home, but at least I had usable transport and I think that's so important for a successful holiday. I can sit here now, writing these words, secure in the knowledge that everything is under control, my car is in capable hands and will soon be as good as new. At last something is starting to go right on this holiday.

When I got back to the Tralee Carapark and Holiday Centre I came across Kathleen reading a book. Thinking I might stimulate a little literary discussion I asked her what she was reading. She handed the book to me. It was called *Canine Orgasm*, and a quick riffle through its pages left me in little doubt about its lubricious contents.

'This is sheer pornography,' I said.

'No it isn't, it's erotica.'

'Oh excuse me,' I said. 'Perhaps you'd care to enlighten me as to the subtle difference.'

'All right,' she said. 'Both pornography and erotica seek to excite the reader, but pornography is masturbatory while erotica is celebratory.'

'You've said a mouthful there,' I remarked.

'Yes. And I want to celebrate.'

I admit that I don't do as much reading as I ought to, but at least I know that I don't, and I know that I ought; and at least when I *do* read it's something decent and improving. Holidays are a great opportunity to catch up. In previous years I've tried *Moby Dick*, *The Decline and Fall of the Roman Empire* and *Orlando Furioso*. This year, by way of a change, I chose *My Family and Other Animals*.

I settled down on the sun-lounger and opened it at the first page. I hadn't got very far when my boy Max happened along. He looked at the title of my book, then said, rather sneeringly, 'My family and other vegetables would be more like it.'

I informed Max that he isn't too old to get a thick ear, and he informed me that he was popping into the next village to have a haircut. I was delighted. I knew he'd feel better for it. Imagine my dismay when he returned from the barber with his head completely shaved.

'Well I suppose it'll save money on shampoo,' I jested.

'Don't be flippant Dad,' he replied. 'Shampoo, haircuts, barbers, they're all symptoms of a bankrupt civilisation.'

'Oh,' I said.

'In a state of nature we'd have none of those things.'

'In a state of nature we'd all have hair down to our knees, crawling with lice.'

He gave me a look as though I'd said something terribly wrong, almost as though I'd betrayed him.

'I'd hoped you might understand,' he said.

Another failure in communication. I felt deeply saddened.

I've got a bit of an idle moment so I've decided to jot down some of my pet hates. This will enable posterity, should posterity ever read this journal, and I must admit I hope that posterity will, to get to know me that little bit better. Who knows, it may even help me to get to know myself. Here goes.

    weathermen
    women who swear
    garlic
    cowboy-boots
    modern art
    Canadians

air pollution
war
people who refer to rugby as rugger
people with dirty fingernails
the hoi-polloi
cardigans
children who call their parents by their first names
desert islands
'Desert Island Discs'
heroin
origami
cocktails
people called Vic
bungalows
all-colour books about the Royal Family
the Royal Family
tandems
famine
people who own exercise-bicycles (exercise-bicycles in themselves I don't mind, it's just the people who own them)
plague
wasting diseases
perversion
self-adhesive envelopes
pencil sharpeners in the shape of other things, like globes and dogs and what have you
the dumping of nuclear waste
veal
Mussolini
Mike Denness
female circumcision
death
paisley
having my eyes tested
rubber gloves
shop assistants of all sorts
vandalism

stamp-collecting
fitted kitchens
ballet
New Year's Eve
fan heaters
tyranny
people with conservatories
conservatories
personal computers
impersonal computers
those little glass balls full of water that you shake and it snows
avalanches
trouser-presses
phlegm
fascism
newspaper ads for wigs where the man is shown before and he's bald and miserable and he's shown after and he's all smiles. If the before man smiled a bit he'd look all right bald and wouldn't need the wig
wigs
cancer
women with hairy armpits
misapplied technology
folk music
record tokens
intolerance
genocide
the fire-bombing of Dresden
people who make their dogs wear overcoats
sweat
bad breath
murder
Nazism
incest
blackmail
emotional blackmail
emotion (when it's misplaced)

violence
gas bills
advertising
Nazism (you just can't say it too often)
neo-Nazism
the New Barbarism
the Old Barbarism
Manchester United (I don't know why but I've never liked them)
death

    I could go on but I've decided to stop there so that I don't give the impression of being a miserable old sod. I began by thinking I'd now make a list of all the things I really like. I put on my thinking cap and came up with truth, beauty and goodness. But then I started asking myself what is truth? What is beauty? What is goodness? Answer came there none. I got fairly introspective and I might have let it get me down if my lovely daughter Sally hadn't happened along and said, 'Why does foolish man stopper his ears to the Word of the Lord?'

    'Don't ask me love,' I said. 'I don't even know why women wear false eyelashes.'

    False eyelashes are another one of my pet hates.

It is after midnight now and the caravan is dark except for a small fluorescent tube by the light of which I'm writing. It's probably a little early in the holiday to start thinking that I've come up with any real wisdom but I've thought of one or two truths that I think are well worth setting down.

    1) never have your house all-electric
    2) buy a good set of carpentry tools – you'll never regret it
    3) plastic surgery is never the real answer

    My flow has just been interrupted by a conversation I've had with my wife Kathleen. She stirred in her sleep and called my name.

    'Eric.'
    'Yes.'
    'Eric.'

'What?'

'Eric.'

'What do you want?'

'I want what you gave me the other night, but I want three times as much.'

'All right. Just let me finish my journal.'

I can't pretend that I'll be entering the marital bunk tonight entirely full of confidence in my ability to meet Kathleen's tripled demands. But nobody will ever be able to say that I'm not a trier.

Tuesday

I was rudely awoken at about six o'clock this morning by the arrival of a police-car flashing its lights and sounding its two-tone horn outside the caravan. I got up, put on my dressing-gown, and was on the point of opening the door to see what all the fuss was about when three policemen, two in plain-clothes, one in uniform, flung the door open. I'd say they used unnecessary force to accomplish this; after all it only has two nails and a bit of string holding it shut. Before I could say, 'What's the meaning of this?' the one in the uniform had got me in an arm-lock and another was waving a truncheon in my face.

The man who didn't have me in an arm-lock and who wasn't waving a truncheon in my face flashed his identity card and I just had time to read that his name was Chief Inspector Hollerenshaw.

He had hair like a Brillo pad and a face that looked as though it had had a Brillo pad used on it. He was broad, heavily built and as hard as they come. He definitely didn't look the sort of man you'd want to cross, the only problem was he behaved as though I'd crossed him. Then he started what can only be described as an interrogation.

'Where were you on the night of the fifth?' he snapped.
'The fifth of what?' I asked, all innocence.
'What?'
'The fifth of which month?'
'That's for me to know and you to find out.'
'I was at home, I suppose.'
'You suppose you were at home yet you don't even know what month I'm talking about.'
'I'm always at home.'
'Whose home?'

'My own home.'

'Oh yes? Who's the strumpet?' and he gestured at Kathleen.

'That's no strumpet,' I said bristling. 'That's my trim and attractive wife.'

'Trim perhaps, but attractive, well that's another matter. Attractiveness is a subjective business, isn't it?'

'Yes,' I said. 'Though I think in Kathleen's case . . .'

I felt my arm being eased out of its socket by the uniformed policeman.

'Isn't it?'

'Yes, yes, it's very subjective.'

'I'm glad we agree. Now where's the stuff?'

'Sorry?'

'I'll give you "sorry"!'

'What stuff?' I pleaded.

'Don't get cute. I have a way of dealing with cute lads.'

He slapped me across the face. It could have been harder but I was glad it wasn't.

'What about the Morrison break-in? Who was your fence? Where's little Victor hanging out these days? What happened to the Old Man? Who's Mr Big?'

'I don't know what you're talking about.'

He slapped me again. Kathleen and the kids were wide awake by now and pretty baffled by what was going on. They didn't help matters much by saying, 'Tell them Dad. For God's sake tell them everything you know.' Still, I suppose they meant well.

'Please,' I said, 'please stop all this nonsense. There's obviously been a mistake.'

'If there's been a mistake then how come you're driving the Wartburg?'

Suddenly light dawned.

'Oh for Pete's sake!' I said, relieved to have found the source of the confusion. 'So that's what this thing's all about. You think I own that car outside, but I don't so it must be a simple case of mistaken identity.'

I explained that I'd only borrowed the car while Honest Iago repaired my own. I was hoping that the mere mention of his name would be enough. I thought the police would probably already know him for a crook and a shady dealer; but they didn't. Neither did they seem at all convinced by my story. Things didn't look very good but nevertheless I like to think that my obvious innocence was shining out.

'All right,' said Hollerenshaw. 'Let's take a ride.'

We piled into the police-car and I directed them along the road that led to Honest Iago's establishment. I sat in the back of the car and was brutalised from time to time by the uniformed man. The driver (the man who'd previously waved the truncheon in my face) drove like a madman. I was tossed around in my seat, my head kept hitting the roof and before long I was experiencing a severe bout of car-sickness.

'Put the radio on,' Hollerenshaw said.

The driver fiddled with the dial and found a news channel.

'I want music, you slag,' Hollerenshaw snarled and tuned the radio himself until he came across something he liked. It was a bit of classical music, just solo piano. It was all right. It didn't do a lot for me but Hollerenshaw seemed transported by it. He got a funny expression on his face, as tears welled in his eyes.

'Mozart,' he said. 'That's what I call music.'

He started to cry like a baby, into a dirty white hanky that the driver handed him. At one point I said, 'I'm sure there's a simple explanation for all this,' but that remark fell on fairly stony ground.

The simple explanation I was hoping for wasn't forthcoming at Honest Iago's. When we arrived at the spot where the garage and used-car lot had been there was now only a heap of demolition rubble and an expanse of cinders. There was certainly no sign of my own car.

We got out of the police-car and paced up and down on the scene of the crime.

'You know why I hate criminals?' Hollerenshaw asked.

'No I don't,' I said.

'Because they're stupid. Know what I mean?'

I nodded.

'I wonder if *you're* stupid. I don't know yet, but I'll give you one piece of advice: – don't get smart with me. Don't get funny with me. All right?'

'All right.'

'I'm the one who's entitled to the laughter, the applause, the public adulation. Right?'

'Right.'

'But do I get it? No. I get abuse, suspicion, hatred. They think I don't know anything about world affairs, the history of ideas. They think I'm ignorant. Ha! What do they know?'

'Nothing,' I said.

'Too right. You think this job's easy you ought to try it. I could have a Merc. I could have a house with a double garage and a greenhouse and a fishpond. I could have a wife who spends afternoons at the solarium and two kids away at boarding-school learning how to become members of the Establishment. But I don't. I don't have any of that. And do you know why?'

'No,' I said.

'Because I'm a thinking copper. Funny that, eh? Big joke wouldn't you say? I want to see you laughing.'

I tried to laugh but it's hard to force mirth when you don't feel like it, and I definitely didn't feel like it. Then he walked over to me, very deliberately, and put his face very close to mine. I could smell garlic on his breath, which is one of my pet hates.

'You know what else?'

I shook my head.

'The funny part about it is, for some reason, I trust you. I don't know why. You must have an honest face.'

Then he spat in my honest face.

'We'll see you again, pal,' the driver of the car said to me.

'Oh well, you know where to find me.'

The three of them got into their car, leaving me standing in the road, cold and inappropriately dressed.

'Any chance of a lift?' I asked.

They all smiled and for a moment I thought they were going to give me a ride back, but instead Hollerenshaw wound down his window and said, 'I'll give you "lift".' And they drove off in a shower of cinders.

It was a long walk back to the Tralee Carapark and Holiday Centre, but it acted as a morning constitutional. Admittedly

I don't normally go for a constitutional in a dressing-gown and slippers and these didn't make the walking any easier. Fortunately it was still early so I didn't meet anyone on the way back, although a van-load of building workers drove past me and jeered. There was also a freak hail-storm but I tried to ignore it.

When I got back to the caravan I discovered that Kathleen had thrown away my breakfast. 'Didn't expect to see you so soon,' she said, 'you old law-breaker.' As she said that I got the distinct impression that she rather liked the idea of my being a law-breaker.

'I'll just have a cup of tea then,' I said.

'We've run out of tea-bags,' she said.

So I trotted along to the site shop to buy some tea-bags. I thought it was fairly remiss of Kathleen to have let us come on holiday without an adequate supply but I said nothing. I sauntered into the shop and was confronted by a sullen youth with a haircut so strange I suppose it must be fashionable. He was reading a newspaper and didn't look up when I entered. When I asked where the tea-bags were he didn't respond, and when I managed to find them and handed him the money to pay for them, he took the money and tossed it into the till without looking at me, the money or the till. All in all he didn't seem a very happy young man.

'Cheer up,' I said. 'It may never happen.'

That remark at least made him look up from his paper. He scowled at me.

'It already has,' he said.

'What's happened exactly?'

'The callous exploitation of unorganised labour.'

'Isn't it always the way?'

'That's a pretty empty response, isn't it?'

I couldn't deny it.

'And in any case it isn't always the way. And even if it is, it doesn't have to be that way. Do you know how much I earn for working in this rat-hole?'

How soon we move from the political to the personal. I said I didn't know how much he earned but I expected it wasn't very much. On the other hand I didn't consider it to be a rat-hole. I thought the shop constituted a pleasant working environment and the job offered an opportunity to serve and meet lots of holidaymakers.

'That has nothing to do with it. I know my worth. I've got talent. My human potential's being criminally wasted in this place. And the pay's rubbish.'

I could see a problem here straight away. Frankly, given the youth's sullenness and unwillingness to oblige I hardly felt he was deserving of a generous salary. On the other hand, perhaps if he was paid more he might be a good deal less sullen and unwilling. It's a problem we often encounter in the bought ledger office.

'You could ask for a raise and resolve to be more cheerful,' I suggested.

'Don't make me laugh,' he replied, laughing ironically.

'Or perhaps you could leave.'

'And do what? Starve?'

'I can see your problem.'

'It's called the cash nexus.'

'I didn't know that.'

'But I see great changes coming. The policies of this retail outlet have become dangerously ossified. The capitalist robber-baron who owns this shop just sits at home all day watching television while I do all the work. If he doesn't bend with the wind of change, then I prophesy a blood-bath.'

'Oh well, I'll watch out for that then,' I said, quite wanting to get back to the caravan for the cup that cheers.

'And when you make yourself some tea with those bags,' he continued, 'just give a thought to the plight of my brothers and sisters among the tea-pickers of Sri Lanka.'

I promised I would.

Later I got to thinking about haircuts and what I'd said to Max about nature. Undoubtedly it's true that if it weren't for a bit of artifice (in the form of shampoo, soap and hairdressing) most of us would look like pigs' breakfasts. Yet when I look at my lovely daughter Sally I always think she's something of a natural beauty. Bit of a paradox here, eh?

While I was having these thoughts I was just staring off into space, or so I thought. In fact it appeared that I was staring rather fixedly at Sally because she asked me, 'Why are you staring at me fixedly?'

'I'm sorry,' I said. 'I was just admiring your natural beauty.'

Another daughter would have been flattered. Not Sally.

'If I have any beauty,' she said, 'it's only because I reflect the beauty of God.'

Kathleen and I are great ones for holiday souvenirs. We enjoy ash-trays, letter-racks, that sort of thing, even a nicely made T-shirt. However, I was a bit surprised when Kathleen suggested that this year, by way of a change, we get ourselves intimately tattooed.

'Pardon?' I said, thinking that I had no desire to have 'A present from Mablethorpe' emblazoned across my chest, much less 'Skegness is so Bracing'.

'I think I'd like an orchid on my buttock,' she said, 'and you can have a bumble-bee.'

I couldn't see the sport in that and I made my feelings plain.

'What's wrong with a trivet?' I asked.

'I don't want a trivet tattooed on my buttock,' she said acidly.

Sometimes I think that woman deliberately tries to misunderstand me.

This whole area is pretty much a haven for fishermen. Every morning you see these complete anglers setting off with their rods and waders and nets. Then twelve hours later they come back with their rods and waders and nets. No fish, just rods and waders and nets. I suppose it might be good for you. Sitting there for twelve hours doing nothing in particular must really clear the mind, assuming that you want your mind cleared. Not everybody does.

Anyway, I was walking along by the river this afternoon, shouting a cheery hello to any anglers I saw, when I came across a pretty unusual sight. One of them had hooked a fish, a pretty lively one at that. The bloke's rod was bending and straining and he was having a rare old tussle. I was reminded of Spencer Tracy.

'Mind if I stand here and watch?' I asked.

The fisherman was engrossed, all the same I thought he might have had the decency to answer me. I don't see why catching a fish means that a chap can't be civil.

The struggle went on for ages and I was getting a bit bored with it, but finally he wound in all his line and the fish was hoisted out of the water still twitching and fighting. It was an ugly little varmint. I'd never seen anything quite like it. It was about the size and shape of a basketball, blue and white striped, with black fins, eyes on stalks, long spiky antennae, and gigantic, sharp, yellow teeth set in a loose, vicious mouth.

I was just about to say, 'There's one to stuff and put on your mantelpiece,' when the creature unhooked itself from the line and went straight for the poor chap's throat. The yellow teeth sank in and the angler writhed around in what looked very much like his death-throes. I was too stunned to do anything. I'm the First-Aid man for our office but the course I did hadn't really prepared me for this sort of lark.

I looked around for a stick or a rock or an emergency telephone, but I was blowed if I could find one.

Not surprisingly, the poor chap who was being attacked fell over, and that caused him to roll down the river-bank and into the water. He was still battling manfully with the fish, but it was an uneven struggle and before long the fish dragged him away from the bank, out into the centre of the river, where the pair of them thrashed for a bit, then slipped out of sight beneath the surface. There were a few bubbles and ripples, but soon all was still and silent.

I looked up and down the river-bank. There were one or two other fishermen visible in the distance, but they were engrossed in what they were doing and I didn't like to disturb them. Besides, what could I have said? 'Beware! The rivers of Lincolnshire are awash with killer-fish the size and shape of basketballs. I know you can't see anything now but one of them just dragged a chap into the river while I stood about and did nothing'? I think not.

I decided it was best not to get involved. I returned to the caravan where Kathleen's lamb and suet surprise was waiting for me.

My lovely daughter Sally has a somewhat creative temperament so I wasn't at all surprised to find her on the sun-lounger with a sketch-pad on her knee. I peered over her shoulder at what she'd been drawing. I'd claim to be a bit of an art-lover but I looked long and hard at what she'd done and I was blowed if I could make head or tail of it.

'What are you drawing there, girl?' I asked, in what I took to be a fatherly manner. 'Is it an abstract or what?'

'It represents the heat death of the universe and the redemptive powers of suffering,' she said. 'But I wouldn't expect you to understand.'

'Just as well!' I snapped back, quick as mustard, but even as I snapped I was saddened that we didn't understand each other better. Why do we always hurt the ones we love?

I was mugged this evening. Hardly what you'd expect in the Tralee Carapark and Holiday Centre. I'd been over to the shower block for a crafty smoke and on the way back was set upon by a couple of lads in rather natty suits. They grabbed me from behind and went through my pockets taking all the money I had. It wasn't much, but enough for a couple of teenage muggers I'd have thought. But no.

'This is no bloody good,' one of them said.

'Well excuse *me*,' I said, in high dudgeon, 'next time I'll make sure I carry enough money to keep the muggers happy.'

He didn't like being talked back to. He kicked me to show his displeasure.

'If we don't get as much money as we need we can turn very ugly.'

Of course, I thought, drugs. No doubt their muggings helped support a serious and costly drug habit. I thought I might as well talk to them about it and see what made them tick.

'What do you spend the money on exactly? Heroin? Cocaine? Pep pills?'

'Don't be silly,' my kicker said. 'We can afford to buy our own drugs. We just do the muggings to pay off our credit cards.'

I suppose this was a sign of the times. Since I didn't have what they considered enough money, they decided to beat me up, 'to teach me a lesson' as they put it. As beatings up go I suspect it wasn't too bad, but I'm really not at all sure what lesson I'm supposed to have learned.

The sullen youth in the shop has given me a lot to think about. When it comes to politics I'd say my views are definitely middle of the road, but 'middle of the road' is a funny expression when you stop to think about it. It's taken to mean moderate and safe, but it all depends which road you're in the middle of. There's nothing very moderate or safe about standing in the middle of the M5.

It's after midnight now, the family is asleep, and I don't feel ready for bed yet so I thought I'd just jot down *My Political Testament*.

> For a start I'm a great believer in freedom so long as one person's freedom doesn't mess up somebody else's. Surely everybody believes that.
>
> At heart I suppose I must be a bit of a capitalist because I quite like the idea of being rich and sitting about doing nothing while the plebs graft away and make money for me. On the other hand I wouldn't much want to be a real pleb and have to graft away just to make a fortune for some capitalist robber-baron. I hate robber-barons as much as the next man; and I don't personally think Communism's such a terrible thing, especially for some of these South American and African types.
>
> Obviously unemployment is a really bad thing, but it's just as obvious that business has to be efficient and lean and not employ people just to stand around. Then if people are unemployed and don't have any

money obviously the State should make sure they don't starve. But if you do too much for people they lose their self-respect and get so that they can't do anything for themselves.

Unions are a very good thing if they protect workers' rights, but a bad thing if they become all militant and subversive.

I think people should be free to walk the streets without being molested by the police, and they should certainly be allowed to sleep in their own caravans, unless of course they're criminals, in which case the police should go in fast and hard. It doesn't pay to have a soft police-force. I think most police are doing a good job but there's always one bad apple and unfortunately I seem to have met him. I'm no fan of capital punishment but how else can you make some people see sense?

I think education's to blame. Everybody's entitled to an education, but sometimes it seems to me that all we're doing is educating people to be unhappy with what they've got. They all think they're so bloody clever. And if the State can't provide a good education then it's only fair to be able to send your kids to public schools so long as they don't turn out a bunch of toffee-nosed snobs and poofs.

I think women should have as many rights as men, but you mustn't forget that men and women are very different. I've no time for these raving feminists, not that I suppose they have much time for me either.

I believe in one man one vote, but I think some people don't know what's good for them. And when you see some of the people they allow to vote it makes you wonder.

I'm sure there are some politicians who are only in it for what they can get out of it, but by and large I expect they mean well and do their best. Personally I wouldn't mind a benevolent dictatorship so long as it was really benevolent. I hate extremists of all persuasions.

I don't really think we should be friendly with countries who are politically wrong, but you can't go interfering with other people's affairs, and if you're too particular you finish up not being friendly with anybody at all.

I don't believe in censorship but sometimes I think things have gone too far, such as in *Canine Orgasm*.

Personally I'd be happy without any nuclear weapons, but when you see some of the crazy foreigners who've got them, then I suppose we'd better have them as well.

I'm sure there are lots of other political hot potatoes I could consider, but that's enough to be going on with. And you see it doesn't seem to me that politics is nearly as complicated as a lot of people like to make out. I think everything I've just written is totally reasonable and I don't see how any sensible person could disagree with any of it. So I don't really understand why there's so much argument.

Good, now that I've got that out of the way I can get on with the real business of living, or in my case sleeping, since I'm about to go to bed; or, since Kathleen will be in bed with me, staying awake for the next hour or two. Ah well, it's only once a year!

Wednesday

There's one thing above all others that puts the icing on the holiday cake for me, and that's a good game of beach-cricket. A holiday simply isn't a holiday without one in my humble opinion. There are some wonderful beach-cricketing moments etched on my memory from previous years; that time in Great Yarmouth when I took a hat trick – Max, Kathleen and Sally sent back to the pavilion in successive balls (admittedly Sally was only six at the time, but still . . .); a splendid knock of eighty-seven I made in poor light at Filey; and a quite devastating caught and bowled to dismiss Kathleen at Bridlington last year, just as she was starting to dominate the bowling.

There's also the joy of seeing the family improve their skills. When I married Kathleen she couldn't bowl so much as an underarm full-toss. Today she bowls lively medium pace and is a joy to watch in the field. Last year she took a sublime catch at gully to dismiss me. Even I had to applaud. In retrospect I realised that I'd got out to a bad shot and I was determined that I wouldn't have a similar rush of blood this year.

We walked to the beach tossing gentle catches to each other. I tried to be encouraging and to boost confidence by shouting 'Well held sir' even if the standard of catching didn't really merit it. We found an empty stretch of beach and I drove the stumps into the sand.

'You bat first, Sally,' I said.

'I'd really just as soon watch,' she said but I wasn't having any of that sort of talk.

Sally took the crease. I sent down the first few balls. It was fairly friendly and Sally managed to get off the mark.

But however friendly the bowling Sally is an irredeemable tail-ender and she played all round the final ball of my over and the leg stump was sent cartwheeling.

Kathleen took the bat. Sally bowled her a steady over. It wasn't great cricket. Kathleen failed to make contact with the ball. Sally failed to make contact with the stumps. I quite fancied my chances with the slower ball and Kathleen lobbed the first delivery of my new over into Max's safe hands. He didn't even have to move.

It was Max's turn to bat. I've often tried to instill into Max the importance of trying to build an innings. Not every ball needs to be hit out of the ground. Picking off singles and twos can be every bit as effective. Today my advice went totally unheeded. I sent down my first ball to him. He charged down the wicket and smashed the ball back over my head. There was no need to chase it. I signalled a six. The next four balls were treated in more or less the same way, with similar savagery and power. The tennis ball flew over the sand and through the air with such regularity that Max had twenty-six runs to his credit by the end of the over.

Sally came on to bowl. I was afraid she'd get a bit of a hammering with Max in his current mood, but to my considerable surprise he played a defensive stroke to each ball. Sally completed a maiden. I don't think she's done that very often.

I returned to the fray. Max played like a boy possessed. The ball shot to every part of the beach, driven, cut, swept, glanced and sometimes just plain slogged, all with absolute authority. I have to admit I was impressed.

I organised a change in the bowling so that Kathleen bowled to Max. He played another six dead-bat strokes. I came on: more mayhem. Kathleen sent down another over: another maiden. I came on again: more fireworks. By the time I'd finished my fourth over Max needed just two runs for his century.

I felt sure that Max's luck must run out sooner or later. A batsman in that mood is bound to attempt an over-ambitious shot sooner or later. I'm sure he could have picked up the runs needed for his century by stroking Kathleen's bowling around, after all she wasn't actually bowling any better than I was, but for reasons at which I can only guess, Max didn't. But the most baffling thing of all happened towards the end of Kathleen's over. She bowled. Max lifted his bat out of the way of the ball and watched as his stumps were demolished.

I had mixed feelings. I'd have liked to see my boy get a century, but for the sake of my bowling analysis I was glad he'd gone. I was sorry he'd got out playing no stroke, but I was sure he'd be the better batsman for it. I suppose I was doubly glad actually because it was now my turn to bat. Max seemed remarkably unconcerned at his dismissal. He showed no disappointment: a true sportsman. He was, in fact, smiling in a self-satisfied way, almost as if he'd got out on purpose.

'Hard lines!' I said.

'It's only a game, Dad,' he replied.

I can't understand that sort of attitude. I took the bat and walked to the crease, loose-limbed and relaxed. I felt in pretty good nick. I was looking to play a long and carefully paced innings.

'Need an umpire?'

I looked behind the bowler's arm and saw the old chap with the radical views on youth. An umpire is a luxury we've seldom had in our beach-cricket but naturally I was delighted to accept his offer. He gave me middle and leg, took six pebbles from the beach to help in counting the overs, and generally looked the part. In fact I couldn't help wondering if he wasn't taking things a little too seriously. He asked me if I wanted to go off for bad light and he warned Sally about running on the pitch, which seemed a little excessive. He also disallowed the first run I scored, claiming it was short. I knew that he was in the wrong but I didn't challenge his authority.

I'd received two overs each from Kathleen and Sally. I'd kept a straight bat, played myself in, and my score had progressed to four. Max kept shouting 'boring', but I'm not the sort of player to be upset by a bit of ill-mannered sledging. I felt in good form. I was seeing the ball early and the sound of willow on tennis ball was rich and resonant. In Sally's next over I played an on-drive straight out of the textbook, then clipped her classically off my legs. Sally simply didn't have any answers.

Max took the cherry. I've long tried to instill into him the virtues of line and length, but it hasn't done much good. He remains wayward. Today he was worse than ever. He developed a lively pace but he sent down a series of long-hops and half-volleys, and a couple of balls that should unquestionably have been called wides by the umpire. I tried to give them the treatment they deserved but I didn't time the ball as sweetly as I'd have liked. Max had one ball left in his over. He came in off a short run and unleashed a vicious 'beamer' at me. And as the so-called ball came at my head I couldn't help noticing that this was not the soft, friendly, yellow tennis ball we'd been using until then, but rather a biggish piece of rock Max had picked up from the beach.

I was rattled. I took my eye off the ball. I raised my bat, more as protection for my head than in any attempt to play a genuine shot. The rock hit the shoulder of the bat, deflected onto my temple and popped up in the air to give Sally an easy catch as she ran in from square leg. To make things worse the blow on the temple caused me to stagger backwards and tread on my stumps.

I looked at the old chap umpiring and was mortified to see that he'd given me out. I thought Max had displayed exactly the kind of youthful behaviour that the old chap would have been so critical of and so eager to stamp out; but all he did was raise his finger.

I might have stood my ground. I might have said that a beamer constitutes intimidatory bowling, should have been declared a no-ball and therefore I shouldn't have been given out. I might also have offered the opinion that pitching a lump of rock at your father's head isn't exactly cricket. But I kept all this to myself. I said nothing. I walked from the crease all quiet decorum. Nobody likes a batsman who can't take his dismissal with good grace.

I'm not the sort of man who makes excuses for his failings on the cricket field, but even apart from the poor umpiring decision I have to say that I've continued to feel one degree under. The summer cold's turned into a real stinker, made all the worse by the blow on the temple. But you won't catch me complaining.

Decided to make the effort and go over and chat with the Garcias, but I've been forced to conclude that they're not really my sort of people.

The sun was barely over the yard-arm but Axel, or Mr Garcia as I prefer to call him, was sitting on the caravan steps swigging liquor from a bottle, something called mescal. He offered it to me, and since I wanted to be friendly I almost accepted. Lucky for me I inspected the bottle and saw there was a dead worm in it. I told him this was precisely the sort of thing I had a phobia about. I said he should return it to the shop and demand a refund. He laughed in that rather mocking way that foreigners do.

Things only got worse when he took a number of tin cans and set them on top of a nearby fence. He then strapped on a holster containing, I had to admit, a rather finely crafted silver revolver. He squinted at the cans through half-closed eyes, then emptied the gun in their general direction. He took a fairly large lump out of the fence but the cans remained pretty much intact. This made him desperately unhappy. He swore horribly in Spanish and stalked off kicking at small children and pets as he went.

Mrs Garcia, whom I had not seen till now, stuck her head out of the caravan and said, 'Has he finished?'

'I think so,' I replied.

She stepped outside. It seemed to me that she was showing a quite needless amount of cleavage for that time of day. I was tempted to ask her to cover herself up, but I expect it would have done little good.

'Axel is not a bad man,' she said, 'but he couldn't hit a tin can from six paces with a machine-gun. He's never found what he wants to do in life. I think he'd be happiest in the medical profession.'

I smiled weakly.

'Well, it's never too late to start a new career,' I said.

Then she placed her hand on my upper arm, threw back her long black hair and said, 'Kiss me amigo.'

I suspect she was having her little joke, but I somehow think that we don't share a similar sense of humour, so to be on the safe side I made my excuses and left. You can't be too careful these days.

I made the discovery today that I'm not the only one keeping a diary. I suppose I shouldn't really be surprised.

It's hard to keep any secrets in a caravan and quite by chance I came across a loose bundle of papers covered in Kathleen's unmistakable handwriting. It seems that her experience of this holiday is a touch different from my own, and that's only to be expected, yet Kathleen's efforts at writing seem so over the top that I can't help wondering if she might need to see a doctor. The prose style is extremely modern and rather overheated. Perhaps she's been influenced by *Canine Orgasm*. It is certainly not family reading but in the interests of completeness I think I'd better give a sample. This is only a tiny snippet. There's plenty more where this came from.

TUESDAY

A telephone rings. On the tongue the taste of honey and lime. Oil on the flesh, a hot sun. The evening wind swirls in from the confines of Asia, olive wood in the hearth, a darkly woven tapestry of lust. We are not strong enough to resist.

The slow awakening of the body, a dark river that stirs in some inner place, becoming white water as it finds the light, seeping through earth, running now down long-parched channels. The odours of flesh and opium, bejewelled hands running over brocade, solitary movements, silent observers, a white neck bruised purple by love, the suitor's tongue, the martyr's kisses, wave-born and pliable as clay.

There is movement beneath the sheets, something human, something fishlike, a heave of loins, a spasm, hair as metal, a pressure, saliva on a finger, jism on velvet, laughter-lines clogged with face-powder.

Somewhere a deal is struck, an assignation, an exchange, a forbidden union of blood and money, intrigue and ecstasy. White wine spills from a rosebud mouth. A heartbeat, trumpets, a skein of sound. Fear, disgust, fascination, the need for violation, the urge for self-debasement. A nipple is stroked to life with a peacock feather. The illusion of completeness. He is merciless. Her body shakes like a wet sheet in the wind.

Long fingers, feline nails lacquered scarlet, a taut foreskin, musk, the air heavy with animals, a moist sound coming from darkness, kohled eyes, black as love, the flavour of peaches, a knife slashing silk.

His body is as smooth as hide, as thick and warm as meat. Sweat glistens on a forehead, at the base of a spine. The bed is deep as a coalmine. Someone sucks her thumb. A spike heel on a marble table, a lean, bare foot strokes a naked cock. The skin is bleached behind a latticework of straps and lacings, a constraint, a liberation. Bare legs on a leather sofa, breasts falling like dough.

Fingermarks, weals, a male silence, an intake of breath. Tongues that lap at an ancient rite, orchids, brandy, the taste of death. The winter grips us. Lean ankles. Jasmine and fennel. Mucus. The whore's boots are stained with ordure. Colours;

cyan, crimson, aquamarine. Faces seen through varnish, a taut puckered sphincter. A tower, its black flag fluttering. Animal horns, flamenco dancers, eels, a sensation of rising, a steel arrow, rage, silver explosions at the corners of vision.

The mist has settled on the shores of the lake. It is dusk. The show is nearly over. Another day ends. We are all alone in our darkness.

I think further comment from me would be superfluous.

Came across my boy Max sitting on the boundary fence of the Tralee, surrounded by stray dogs and lost cats. As I watched he seemed, literally, to charm the birds out of the trees. Sparrows, crows, blackbirds and thrushes descended from the branches and settled on his shoulders and on the fence. Rabbits popped up out of the grass. Squirrels appeared. Foxes, mice, badgers, weasels, all joined the throng and settled around Max. He looked more at home than he had when playing cricket. I was slightly stunned.

'What are you up to Max?' I shouted, which had the unfortunate effect of scaring off much of the wildlife.

'I was talking to the animals,' he replied.

'Talking?'

'Just talking,' he said. 'They speak my language. Though sometimes I think talking isn't enough.'

I didn't argue with him.

If I'm a good father, and without boasting I like to think that I am, I put it down to the fact that I have a good long memory. I can remember quite clearly what it was like to be a child, a schoolboy or an adolescent.

Ah adolescence! It's the best of times and the worst of times. All those new chemicals and hormones start pulsing through your bloodstream, and even though it's pretty exciting, it's pretty painful and confusing too.

And what makes adolescence particularly poignant is the

way that certain things about it stay with you for the rest of your life; certain enthusiasms, certain places, a certain song or book; or in my case Joan Crawford.

Every healthy, growing lad has a favourite pin-up (although I can't say that Max has) and for lads of my generation the choice wasn't easy. We were spoiled for choice. There was Marilyn Monroe, Jane Russell, Liz Taylor, but I always found them a bit obvious. There was Natalie Wood, Shirley MacLaine, Debbie Reynolds, but they were never obvious enough. There was even Diana Dors, but she was English, and being English is always a drawback for a pin-up. I wanted someone more worldly, sophisticated, mature, even if it meant picking someone who was a bit long in the tooth. So I picked Joan Crawford.

While the other lads queued up for *Some Like It Hot*, *Giant* or *The Girl Can't Help It* I was handing over my money to see *Johnny Guitar* and *The Story of Esther Costello*. While they were packing in to *Bus Stop* and *Rebel Without a Cause* I was searching out rare showings of *Strange Cargo*, *Grand Hotel* and *Mildred Pierce*. I think the other lads probably thought I was a bit strange, but even then I wasn't afraid to march to the beat of a different drummer.

I find it fairly hard to say just what Joan had that really hits the spot for me. Of course she was sexy and statuesque, but who wasn't in those days? Of course she had flashing eyes, a finely chiselled nose with flaring nostrils, and a warm, melting mouth. She was distinguished, determined, passionate, perhaps a little haughty. But she had something more than all of these. She had *class*. She was also something of an icon.

In later years it was revealed that Joan had appeared in blue movies before she got her big break. That didn't exactly gild the lily but I never held it against her. It only made me feel a deep compassion for her; and it proved, as if proof were necessary, that above all else Joan was a survivor.

Then it came out that Joan was less than the ideal parent

and beat her daughter with a wire coat-hanger. Also, of course, she did get a bit ugly towards the end and her face turned into a sort of Joan Crawford mask, all big lips and arched eyebrows; and she married the chap who was chairman of Pepsi-Cola, and she started appearing in terrible American soap operas. But it didn't matter to me. If it had been revealed that she was a drug-pusher, a mass murderer, a white-slaver, it wouldn't have made any difference as far as I was concerned. I could forgive Joan anything.

I only mention Joan Crawford at this point because I never go anywhere without taking a large coffee-table volume of portraits of her. I mean I go to work or to the DIY shop, but two weeks away without a glimpse of Joan would be unthinkable. When life's getting me down, as it was at various times today, I just open my book, turn its heavy, glossy pages, and in no time at all I'm feeling like my old self. Sometimes I feel better than my old self. I feel ennobled and elevated. That's the way it is with icons.

As a family we've always found nudity to be natural and healthy without making a big thing of it. Imagine my surprise however, on emerging from the caravan, to find my lovely daughter Sally prostrate, arms outstretched along the ground, legs together (I'm pleased to say), and naked but for a pair of burgundy slingbacks and a lot of suntan oil.

I felt I had to say something. I suggested to her that her appearance might cause embarrassment and offence to our friends the Garcias, but I couldn't make her see my point of view. In the end I just said, 'What the hell do you think you're doing?'

'I am making my body a temple for Christ,' she said.

I couldn't come up with a reply to that so I kept my peace. I'm sure she'll grow out of it, but I hope it's soon.

Tried to make myself a cup of tea and discovered that we've now run out of sugar. Again I thought Kathleen had been remiss, but I'll admit that my boy Max has been getting through a lot more sugar than usual. He probably needs it. He's been burning up a lot of energy lately.

So I trotted along to the site shop hoping to find the sullen youth in better spirits than when I last saw him. Certainly he was more animated and he displayed none of his old unwillingness to make eye contact. He was blocking the door to the shop. His hair looked stranger than ever, and he was brandishing a placard that read, 'Support the wildcat strike, a small gesture in the struggle for workers' rights and world equality. Death to the exploiters.' It was a fair-sized placard.

'Does this mean I can't buy a packet of sugar?' I enquired.

'I'm glad my political message is getting across.'

'Oh it is,' I said. 'In fact I took to heart what you said about the tea-pickers in Sri Lanka. I've given their plight some serious attention. I've been thinking about nothing else.'

This was a fib, but I thought it was justified since I was buttering up the sullen youth in the interests of a greater good.

'In fact I've reconsidered my whole political stance,' I added.

'The time for reconsideration is passed. What I want is confrontation.'

'Does this mean there's no point trying to reason with you?'

'Right.'

This is what I hate about politics. What's the point of *my* being reasonable if nobody else is going to be? However much I wanted my sugar I really didn't fancy a confrontation with the youth. I knew Kathleen wasn't going to be very pleased when I came home empty-handed, but even she can't argue with political necessity.

It's after midnight now. Frankly it's been a very full day and I feel considerably too worn out to be really philosophical. I also feel worn out just thinking about what the night ahead with Kathleen holds. I've already noted that I can't deny her anything, and even if I tried to deny her I suspect she wouldn't let me.

I suppose I shouldn't complain. A lot of men would give an arm and a leg to find themselves in my position, with a wife who still finds me irresistible after all these years of marriage. And I can't resist *her* either, though God knows I try.

Thursday

I awoke in the middle of a night of anxious and exhausting dreams to feel a strange, looming presence. I switched on my bunkside light and found my lovely daughter Sally standing over me. Her hair was wild, her nightgown loose, and she was holding a Bible, rosary beads and a phial of what might very well have been Holy Water. I try to be an understanding father but this was beyond a joke.

'What time do you call this?' I asked, not altogether relevantly.
'The witching hour,' she said.
I wished I'd never asked.
'And what exactly do you think you're up to, young lady?'
'I'm praying for you father.'
I was speechless.
'I know you're not a bad man, father, but you've fallen prey to the wiles of Satan.'
'I most certainly have *not*!'
'Don't worry father. I'll try to intercede with the Godhead.'

And with that she returned to her own bed. This morning I wondered if it had all been a dream. At the very least I thought Sally might have been sleep-walking. Over black pudding and scrambled egg at breakfast neither of us referred to it. It didn't seem like the time to play the heavy father.

Set off on my morning constitutional and soon fell in step with the cheery old gent from the Tralee who had radical views on youth and had acted as our umpire. He was in a sunny mood and we talked nine to the dozen about ballroom dancing, the state of our universities, handguns, fashions in swimwear, and the gold standard. Again his views were lively but perfectly reasonable, and when the conversation turned to cricket I saw no reason why I shouldn't mention the matter of my dismissal in yesterday's cricket match.

'I'm not calling you incompetent or anything,' I said, 'but the way I see it Max's bowling was clearly intimidatory and therefore . . .'

His face turned scarlet. So did his eyes.

'I don't give a spit how you see it,' he shouted.

'Now don't get . . .'

'I don't give a monkey's giblet for you or your opinions. The umpire is the final and only arbiter of fair and unfair play, and anyone who wants to argue about it is very likely to get a cricket bat doused in petrol shoved up his rectum, and I personally will be only too happy to put a match to it.'

I've always known it was wrong to question the umpire's decision, now I knew it better than ever. I now also know that the old chap's radical views extend beyond the subject of youth.

'You're right of course,' I said.

The old chap smiled and regained his composure.

'Actually, the main reason I didn't no-ball Max,' he said, 'was that he looked such a vicious great brute I was afraid he might knock my teeth out.'

I'd parted company with the old chap and was reaching the end of my constitutional when I came across a bloke who asked me to buy some raffle tickets from him. I always enjoy helping a good cause and this was in aid of animal welfare so I took half a dozen tickets off his hands.

'What can I win?'

'Prizes galore,' he said. 'The holiday of a lifetime, saucepan sets, travelling alarm clocks. All sorts.'

Not that I supposed it made much difference what the prizes were. I'd never won anything in my life. I'm just not lucky that way. However, less than fifteen minutes later a blue van drew up at the caravan, the bloke who'd sold me the tickets got out and congratulated me on having won a major prize.

'Don't tell me,' I said, staggered. 'It's the holiday of a lifetime, isn't it?'

'No, it's not as major as that. You've won a dog.'

He opened the back door of his van to reveal a big, black animal snarling at me from the darkness inside. 'Come on Sinbad,' the bloke said, and the dog slunk out. He was a handsome beast I suppose. He was as big as a small horse and had a bit of Alsatian in him, also a bit of Rottweiler I think, a hint of Great Dane, and judging from appearances a fair helping of wolf. He didn't seem a happy dog. The sinews in his throat were taut as piano wires, the eyes were livid, and a trail of white foam spilled from his open mouth. I don't even want to describe the teeth. He wore a vast, studded collar attached to a piece of chain, and the man now thrust the chain into my hand.

'I'm not a dog person,' I protested, but the bloke wasn't listening. He was in his van, accelerating away.

The dog and I looked at each other. It wasn't love at first sight. All I could think of was to get the animal to a police-station, explain my predicament, and at the very least get them to take Sinbad to the RSPCA. I only hoped that Hollerenshaw wasn't going to be at the station.

But my plans in that direction didn't get very far. I held the chain firmly and tugged in the direction I wanted the dog to go. The dog didn't want to go anywhere that I wanted to. We had a short battle of wills which ended when Sinbad let out a blood-piercing howl, snapped his jaws at me and knocked me over. The chain fell from my hand and the dog bounded away, barking like a hound from hell.

It appeared that his bite was every bit as bad as his bark. He ran round the site terrorising children, wounding smaller dogs (though I'm sure he'd have wounded larger dogs too, had there been any), knocking over picnic tables and barbecues, finally leaping over a fence into an adjacent field where he savaged a number of sheep. Several caravanners were a bit upset by it all and I couldn't blame them.

All morning howls and barking drifted towards the Tralee. One brave soul who claimed to be good with animals went to win Sinbad's confidence, but had his trouser-leg bitten off and came back looking crestfallen. The dog then took up position by the entrance to the site and sat very quietly, only breaking out into terrifying savagery if anybody came within twenty-five yards of him or attempted to enter or leave.

I knew it was an unsatisfactory situation and I thought I had a duty to sort it out. The dog was after all, in a sense, reluctantly, mine. I got half a pound of sausages from our caravan and went to tempt Sinbad. I tried to look friendly. I tried not to show fear. I managed quite well at first. I think I didn't even show fear when he started sprinting towards me, but a second later he'd swallowed the sausages and had my hand gripped between his jaws, by which time it didn't seem to make much difference whether I showed fear or not.

He wasn't biting the hand that fed him exactly. He was just clenching his teeth round it, thereby stopping the blood supply, and chewing it from time to time. At least it prevented him barking, though he could still let out a fairly nasty growl.

We stayed like that for some time and could probably have been there now, with gangrene starting to set in, if Max hadn't arrived on the scene. I don't know where he'd been, probably on one of his nature rambles. Sinbad let go of my hand when he saw Max, ceased the growling and renewed his barking and howling. He lunged at Max, his teeth bared, his eyes an unnatural yellow. Max was very calm. He looked the animal straight in the eyes, then unleashed a mighty uppercut that snapped the dog's head up and back. Sinbad hit the ground unconscious.

I started to thank Max but he waved away my gratitude.

'You see,' he said, 'sometimes talking to them isn't enough.'

He bent over the dog and took one of its rear paws in his hands. He held it up so I could see there was a large thorn impaled in the soft flesh. Max removed it.

When the dog came to Max patted him lovingly on the head. Sinbad made a sound very like purring. He looked as playful and as docile as a puppy but I must say there was something in his eyes that told me the old brutality wasn't gone forever. I've never trusted dogs.

A group of holidaymakers watched in some amazement as Max and Sinbad walked out of the Tralee Carapark and Holiday Centre together. They made a fine pair. A boy and his dog. It did my old heart good, but I'm still not a dog person.

My hand didn't look very good when Sinbad had finished with it. I probably wouldn't have worried about it myself but Kathleen insisted that, just to be on the safe side, she'd take me along to the local casualty department. I thought that was unusually caring of Kathleen.

We got to the waiting-room and announced ourselves at the desk. The bloke behind the said desk squinted insolently at my hand but didn't seem very impressed by it. He told us to take a seat and someone would be with us as soon as possible. I didn't find that terribly reassuring. 'Someone' could be anyone. It would have put my mind far more at ease if he'd said, 'A first-rate, highly competent doctor will see you'. It's all a question of public relations.

Hieronymus Bosch has never been one of my favourite painters but I'm sure he could have done a very good job of depicting what things were like in that waiting-room. The place was packed with people, most of them displaying some unattractive symptom: wounds, cuts, watery eyes, swellings, arms and legs bent into impossible positions, running sores, to name but a few. It all made me feel pretty ill. And as background detail to all this there were weeping relations, a few drunks, people being sick, men pacing the room, children playing on the floor with Lego, getting bored with that then chasing each other and screaming.

We waited an hour or so. I tried to read a magazine. Kathleen chatted happily with doctors, porters, male nurses and maintenance men. She said it helped to pass the time. But eventually my turn came and I was shown into a large inner room, subdivided into cubicles by green curtains. 'Lie down on the bed and someone will be along in a minute.' Someone again. I tried to get comfy on the thin bed.

From the other side of my cubicle's curtain I could hear a woman weeping. 'You all right in there?' I called cheerily.

There was no answer, unless you call more weeping an answer. I thought I'd better have a look so I peeped through a gap in the curtains. I saw a pretty horrific spectacle.

The weeping was coming from a stout, dowdy old woman who was sitting on a chair clasping the hand of a male figure laid out on the bed. She was inconsolable. The man was motionless. He was soaked in sweat, dirt and blood. Bits of his body were wrapped in filthy bandages and his clothes were in tatters. His skin was unnaturally white and covered in scratches and bruises. Then I looked more closely (and it was a second or two before I took it in properly) and I saw that he'd been decapitated. The old woman was holding hands with a headless corpse. No wonder she was a bit cut up.

'Cheer up love,' I said. 'Worse things happen at sea.'

She was lost for words. I could see her struggling to speak but it was a long time before anything came out. Finally she said, 'I wouldn't mind. But he only came in with indigestion.'

I could hear footsteps approaching so I stuck my head back into my own cubicle. I can't say I was filled with confidence. If they chop your head off when you've only got indigestion, what are they likely to do if you come in with a bad hand? I heard someone talking to the old woman. Then the body was wheeled away and the weeping receded with it. I heard another patient being wheeled in as a replacement. There were two male voices now, clipped efficient, using lots of medical words. Doctors, I supposed. Chains rattled. There was an electronic hum, then the noise of sawing, chopping, splintering, a loud splash of liquid, and a noise as though someone had thrown a huge piece of liver down onto a slab. My hand was feeling better all the time.

The voices became more audible. One of them said, 'But do we have the right to play God?' 'Of course we bloody do,' said the other.

I decided to make a quick exit. As I was stepping from my cubicle a passing nurse grabbed me. 'Ah yes,' she said, 'you'll be here for the operation. Walk this way.'

She dragged me towards some swing doors through which I could see an operating theatre. There were two greasy, unshaven oafs in dungarees and wellingtons lounging about in there. They were eating fried chicken and fiddling with evil-looking bits of medical equipment. They gave me ugly smiles and beckoned me in.

I pulled away from the nurse. 'No, no,' I said, 'I think there's been some kind of mistake. There's nothing wrong with me. I'm just here to read the meter.'

I don't think she entirely believed me but she hesitated for a second and that was enough for me to escape her attentions and return to the waiting-room. She didn't pursue me. No doubt she had other things to do. Nurses are busy people. The waiting-room hadn't improved. I found Kathleen making friends with a group of student doctors. She left them reluctantly and we went back to our car.

'What did they say?' she asked.

'Oh, nothing to worry about,' I said casually. 'I've just got to take it easy.'

'Not too easy I hope. I trust you'll be fit and active for this evening.'

I had a sudden relapse.

I really needed a cigarette after all this nonsense and I'm sure there are many wives who would have capitulated and allowed me, in the exceptional circumstances, to have a quick smoke in my own caravan. But Kathleen is made of sterner stuff, so I had to go to the shower and toilet block as usual.

I stood by the sinks, lit up, and looked at myself in the mirror. Unless I'm very much mistaken I have rather more grey hairs today than I did a week ago. Ah well, I don't think there's any point trying to hide these things. Perhaps I'll become distinguished with age.

As I was thinking that, the door to one of the stalls flew open and a large, grey, demented figure leapt at me. It was Chief Inspector Hollerenshaw again. He seized me by the neck with one hand, pushed my head down into one of the sinks, while his other hand turned on both hot and cold taps. The sink filled. My head was drenched. One ear had a torrent of icy water directed at it and the other ear was scalded by the hot. Water went up my nose and down my throat, and I wondered briefly if I were going to drown. But that was not Hollerenshaw's plan. He pulled my head out of the sink and threw me across the room.

'You know what *I* think?' he said.

I couldn't speak. I just shook my head and looked at him in a receptive manner.

'I think people who aren't ready for the responsibility of owning dogs shouldn't be allowed to have them. Oh yes, I know people like you. You think they make cute, lovable, Christmas presents. Well I'm here to tell you that they're a lot more than that. They're living, breathing creatures. They need commitment and love. I think that people who don't look after their dogs properly are sad, inadequate scum. I think society could get along just fine without people like that.'

I tried to protest. I tried to explain about the raffle, and the man in the van, and the thorn in the paw, but I couldn't really get a word in edgeways.

'I'll give you "raffle",' Hollerenshaw continued. 'I had a dog once, when I was a boy. He was the best friend I ever had. We went everywhere together. Did everything together. I just whistled and he obeyed me without question. He was called Wolfgang.'

Hollerenshaw began to whistle a snatch of classical music, by Mozart no doubt, very, very loudly. As he whistled he began to sob.

'Where did I go wrong? I'm not a bad man,' he said between whistles and sobs. 'But nobody obeys when I whistle now. I'm too sensitive for this job you know. I'm too empathetic. I see both sides, every side. I think we're all guilty. I think too much. You've got to help me, Eric. Please.'

I did my best. I whistled along with him as best I could. I told him it would probably all look very different in the morning. I like to think I was some small help. If there was one thing I learned today it's that however black things look there's always a policeman somewhere who's worse off than you.

Max returned for the evening meal. He was alone.

'What happened to Sinbad?' I asked.

'I gave him his freedom,' said Max. 'He's returned to the wild.'

He never seemed to have been very far from the wild as far as I could see. The removal of the thorn may have left him happy and less murderous than he was, but that still leaves him murderous enough for most purposes. I hope Hollerenshaw doesn't get to hear about it.

After dinner I felt I needed something to take my mind off my worries, and I do enjoy playing games, be they indoor or outdoor, but after my recent experiences playing beach-cricket I thought it best to stick to the indoor variety. I'm not a highly competitive person. I don't particularly care whether I win or lose. I like games because they're character-building and a great civilising influence, especially for young people. Certainly they're much better for the mind and body than is lounging around watching television (unless of course there's a Joan Crawford film showing).

The rest of the family have never really shared my enthusiasm and this evening I had a hard time persuading anyone to play anything. I've brought a wide variety of board games with us, something for everyone I'd have thought, but I couldn't find any takers.

'Come on Dad,' said Max, 'Cluedo and Monopoly are all right, but they're kids' stuff. I want to play something with a bit more risk and challenge.'

'Such as?'

'A truth game.'

I'd never heard of such a thing, but I was so keen to play some sort of game that I agreed to give it a whirl. Max briefly explained the rules. Frankly I can't ever see it catching on but what happens is this: each player has to reveal some dark secret about himself or herself that until now has been kept hidden from the other players. And that's all there is to it! Sounds too easy, doesn't it?

'But how do you know whether you've won or lost?' I enquired.

'You know all right,' Max said menacingly.

So we gave it a go. I set the ball rolling by confessing that when I sold the old Ford Escort to that nice Mrs Henderson,

I told her I'd had a new gearbox put in. That was a lie. The gearbox was only reconditioned.

I must say I've always felt a bit guilty about that, and as a matter of fact I did feel better for having got it off my chest. I began to see that there might be something in this truth game. Max, of course, wasn't very impressed by my revelation.

'We're looking for something a bit more fundamental,' he carped. 'Something that really strikes at the roots.'

'Like what?'

'Say if you were a war criminal or something.'

I gave Max what I like to think of as my withering look. Max didn't wither.

'If you're so clever Max, let's see you come up with something,' I challenged, but I soon wished I hadn't.

Max said, 'The truth is I want to kill you Dad, and sleep with Mum.'

I laughed nervously but I knew things had gone beyond a joke. That isn't the sort of sentiment a man expects to hear in his own rented caravan. I looked to Kathleen hoping for a bit of wifely support, but, to my chagrin, Kathleen (not usually the most willing games player) had decided to enter into the spirit of the thing.

'If it's really cards on the table time,' she said, 'there is one thing I've never told anybody.'

I felt briefly relieved. It meant that at least she wasn't going to say she wanted to be had by an Arab with a big tool who really knew how to use it, since she had already told me that. But my relief was misplaced.

'It's always been my fantasy,' she continued, 'to be rogered simultaneously by two well-endowed dwarves, one at each end.'

'Mother!' I said involuntarily.

She hates it when I call her Mother. Trust Kathleen to enter into the spirit when spirit isn't required. I was nonplussed. As Max so rightly said, you certainly knew when you were losing at this game. Who knows how things might have turned out if my lovely daughter Sally hadn't entered the fray.

'The only Truth is the Lord's,' she said, 'and that is no game.'

That put a most welcome damper on things. It'll be a long time before you catch me playing truth games again.

It is after midnight now and my head is full of many things: cricket umpiring, dogs, raffles, hospitals, police harrassment and sex. Let me say right off that I like sex as much as anybody. All right, perhaps not *absolutely* anybody, but I like it well enough. Enough for me, anyway. And I'm sure that most people find when they're on holiday that they relax, they have more time for their partner, they think about sex a little more often than they do at home. Certainly this is the effect our holiday's had on Kathleen.

It would be nice to say that Kathleen has been very loving on this holiday, but I'm not sure that 'loving' is quite the right word, 'demanding' is a bit more like it. And if I'm honest I must say that it doesn't seem to me that Kathleen's demands have been motivated by love or affection, more by some uncontrollable form of sexual mania.

I realise now that it started almost the moment we arrived here, and it certainly hasn't got any better since. As soon as we arrived at the Tralee she pointed out some young man in shorts who was walking past the caravan and said, as I now bitterly recall, 'Look at the pork sword on him. That's what I call monster meat!' Naturally I didn't bother to look and I didn't think much of it at the time. I certainly didn't bother to mention it in my journal, but in retrospect it does seem to have been a bit of a harbinger.

I began by thinking that if I gave Kathleen what she wanted she'd be happy and then settle down a bit. But no. I like to think that in the beginning I gave her pretty much what she asked for, but then, like Oliver Twist, she asked for more. So I've been trying to give her more, but it hasn't been easy and I gather from certain rather caustic remarks she's made that I've left her wanting, and it now seems to me that she wants more than any decent man can provide. I'm not saying that Kathleen's insatiable. I'm sure a hand-picked team of fit and highly trained young studs could satisfy her. The problem is that I'm not a team.

I tried this evening to discuss the matter and get across my point of view.

'I'm forty-five years old Kathleen. I do my best but you've got to remember I'm at least twenty-five years past my sexual peak.'

Her reply, which I'm only writing down in the interests of giving a complete account, was, 'If you can't shit then get off the chemical toilet.'

I don't know exactly what she meant by that. It just sounds like another example of the coarseness Kathleen is so keen on these days. As I write, she is stirring in the bunk and I will soon be called upon to fulfil my husbandly duty. Many are called but I seem to be the one who's chosen.

Friday

More freak weather today. I was returning from the shower block after a much needed smoke when the sun disappeared and the whole of the Tralee Carapark and Holiday Centre became enshrouded in an impenetrable fog. It was a real pea-souper. I could barely see as far as the next caravan. Nevertheless, I decided to go on my constitutional. I didn't see a soul. I suppose they had fainter hearts than me.

Then suddenly I *did* see something. I know the old eyes can play strange tricks in the fog, yet I swear I saw a masked, male figure, dressed in pirate boots and a loin-cloth, dragging a lifeless body through the site to a spot where a shallow grave had been recently dug. The body was dumped in the grave and the masked man rapidly flung earth over it.

There were two things that struck me as interesting about this. One, although the person doing the dragging and burying was masked, and dressed in an uncharacteristic outfit, I swear he had a look of Axel Garcia about him. Two, the corpse was headless.

Then the fog lifted, the sun reappeared and it was a beautiful morning. There was no sign of Garcia, the headless corpse or the shallow grave. I felt a bit of a clot. It's always been said that I've got a bit of an imagination, and perhaps I was still a bit disturbed after yesterday's experience at the hospital, so I shrugged it off. I concluded that it must have been a trick of the light.

The labour relations at the site shop have been preying on my mind slightly. Unwilling to be inconvenienced by a little local political unrest I sent my boy, Max, out to the shop in a second attempt to buy some sugar. I had two reasons for doing this.

First, Max is about the same age as the sullen youth, so I hoped they might establish a rapport, at least enough of one to enable Max to procure the sugar. Secondly, Max is a fairly fearsome sight these days. He's taken to wearing animal skins and his behaviour is, to say the least, unsophisticated. If the rapport didn't work I thought he might well be able to frighten the youth into doing a bit of trade.

Max set off willingly enough, which is unusual for Max, but when he hadn't returned after an hour I decided to go and see what had happened to him. I sincerely hoped that he hadn't become enmeshed in an ugly dispute, but I hoped in vain.

Max and the sullen youth had certainly established a rapport. So much so that Max had joined the picket-line. The youth still had his sign about workers' rights and world equality, while Max had a smaller one that read, 'Natural Justice – or else'.

'Max,' I said, offering a bit of fatherly advice, 'I'm all for a bit of awakening political consciousness in a teenage lad but this isn't getting us any sugar, is it?'

Max produced a Bowie knife and held it to my throat. I was taken aback, but not nearly so much as I was when the sullen youth locked his arm round my neck and held a bottle of bleach inches from my face.

'Are you with us or against us?' the youth demanded.

'I don't think I can answer a simple yes or no to a question like that,' I said.

But the sullen youth wasn't interested in half measures or reasoned discussion, and so it was that I became a political hostage. The youth's demands didn't actually seem all that outrageous to me. All he wanted was a pay rise of ten pounds a week, and if he didn't get it I got concentrated ammonia in my eyes.

I know that in a perfect world we shouldn't give in to threats and blackmail but you feel a bit less hardline about that sort of thing when it's *your* eyes that are at stake. I offered to phone the owner of the shop and explain the situation. I hoped the whole thing could be sorted out over beer and sandwiches.

I made the phone call. I got the owner's wife. I asked her to put her husband on but she said she didn't dare disturb him since he was watching a Rita Hayworth film on daytime television. I could understand his reluctance to talk on the phone. Perhaps he felt the same way about Rita Hayworth as I do about Joan Crawford. But after a lot of pleading the wife agreed to put him on. I told him how things were at the shop and he admitted that something needed to be done. He agreed to come along to the shop and discuss the situation just as soon as the film finished. To be honest I don't think he cared greatly about my eyes, but he did seem concerned that the shop was closed and therefore not making any money.

'See what I mean,' the sullen youth said. 'An out and out capitalist robber-baron.'

When the owner arrived he didn't look much like a robber-baron. He looked more like an old buffer who shouldn't be allowed to run a whelk stall, let alone a shop on the Tralee Carapark and Holiday Centre. Nevertheless, when it came to wage-negotiation he was a tough customer.

'Can you put a price on a man's sight?' the sullen youth demanded.

'Yes,' said the owner. 'About an extra five quid a week. And that's as far as I'm prepared to go.'

It looked like deadlock. 'Surely we can come to a compromise on this,' I said. Neither party could see how, but fortunately I came up with a face-saving plan. The owner agreed to pay the sullen youth an extra five pounds a week and I agreed to make up the extra fiver out of my own pocket. It seemed a small price to pay. A deal was struck and we all shook hands. The owner hurried back to his TV while the youth opened the shop. Isn't it a shame that all disputes can't end as happily as this one?

I bought a bag of sugar. As we returned to the caravan Max assured me that if it had come to it he wouldn't have let the sullen youth throw bleach in my face.

'That's good to know, Max. I've always suspected that you were a good-natured boy at heart.'

He seemed pleased by my compliment. He let out a whoop of delight and scurried off into the distance. I returned to the caravan and had a much needed cup of tea: white with two sugars.

The tea helped but I was still feeling in need of a bit of succour. I thought I'd spend half an hour quietly with Joan Crawford. I put the coffee-table volume in my lap and started to riffle through her pages. And then I felt an icy stab in my heart. Joan has been desecrated. Someone has been at work with an evil intent and a felt-tipped pen.
In a still from *Susan and God* Joan now sports a bushy beard and handlebar mustache. Her gypsy madonna good looks are defiled in a portrait from *Forsaking All Others* by the addition of little round glasses and a wicked dose of acne. In *No More Ladies* Joan's perfectly ample though by no means excessive cleavage has been crudely increased, while an unwanted speech bubble has been attached to her mouth in a shot from *They All Kissed the Bride*. The bubble contains the words, 'And that's not all they did.' And so it goes on, page after page of juvenile scribbling and crude annotation. I felt sick to my stomach. More than that I was furious. I ranted and raved, cursed the villain who'd done this and wished that he might rot in hell. I felt pretty immoderate.
Of course, Max was my prime suspect but he was off in the distance. Kathleen couldn't see what I was fussing about, which certainly didn't help; and, in the middle of all this, Sally happened along and said, 'Well Dad, if you *will* worship graven images . . .' She was surprised when this made me more furious than ever.

Treated to another aerial display. The earlier stunt flying of the old Sopwith Camel had been exhilarating enough, but today we saw how it was done in World War Two, and it left me breathless.
A yellow-nosed Messerschmitt 109 dived at us out of the sun. As it approached I could hear what sounded like anti-aircraft fire; a clever sound effect no doubt. The plane levelled off as it reached the Tralee, kept exceptionally low, and began strafing the site. I must say I was a little surprised to find them using

real bullets, but no doubt these air circus folk are sticklers for realism.

Suddenly the cockpit of the plane filled with smoke and I saw oil gush all over the windscreen and the engine cowling. The plane hurtled out of sight, its engine screaming like a banshee and dropping vital bits as it went. After a while there was a distant, almighty explosion.

Fortunately there was no real damage done to the Tralee, although the personable young chap with the stutter had his lilo riddled. I told him he should pop along to the airfield and demand compensation, or at least free tickets to the show, but he's probably too unassuming for that. It's a hard world for people like him.

I also couldn't help noticing that there was a line of bullet-holes in the roof of the Wartburg. If it were my own car I'd probably be fairly upset about that. Since it's somebody else's I'm not too bothered. It's an ill wind . . . And of course it was all very historic and highly educational, especially for the young, once again.

You know I've always had a bit of a soft spot for history. Maybe it's because I'm a bit behind the times and not really a man of today, but whatever the reason I've always been fascinated by those old historical chestnuts like: 'Who was Jack the Ripper?' 'Why did the Light Brigade charge?' 'Who moved the stone?' 'Why wasn't Ethelred ready?'

The main problem I find with history is, that by and large, it isn't full of very nice people. It's full of murderers, power-mad despots, warmongers, zealots, bigots and fruitcakes, not my type at all. In fact there are an awful lot of historical figures I'd like to give a piece of my mind to. I've compiled a list of these with, where appropriate, notes as to what I might say.

>Rasputin
>Tiberius
>Elvis Presley
>Peter the Great (I really don't have much time for anyone who insists on calling himself 'Great'. Why not go for Peter the Modest and leave it to others to decide just how great you were?)

Mussolini (Never trust a national leader who wears an absurd uniform.)
Henry VIII
Ulysses Simpson Grant
Pablo Picasso ('Hello Mr Picasso,' I'd say. 'A child of three could have done these paintings!' Actually I don't think that's true, but I'd say it anyway, just to annoy him. I don't know why, but I've never liked him. I think it's got something to do with the shape of his head.)
Jesse James (What kind of name is Jesse for an outlaw?)
Mozart
Dr Crippen
Chairman Mao (Never trust a national leader who wears an absurd boiler-suit either.)
Sigmund Freud (At least he'd know what to do with a piece of my mind!)
Helen of Troy (All right, so her face launched a thousand ships, so what? What's so great about launching ships? And how do you launch a ship with your face anyhow?)
George Formby
Christopher Columbus
Dr Johnson ('I wonder if you'd mind having a look at my leg?')
And finally the Earl of Sandwich (I'd point out what a good job it is that he wasn't called Pratt or Sidebottom or we'd all be going around eating toasted sidebottoms and cheese and pickle pratts. Although, of course, *I* wouldn't unless Kathleen had made them with her own fair hand.)

Ah well, so much for whimsy! At least it's good to see I haven't lost my sense of humour!

I decided I'd really have to talk to Sally about this whole religion business. There are times when a father should stay out of things but there are other times when he has to leap right in. Sally might not like what I had to say, but one day she'll thank me for it. I found her in the children's playground. She had a gang of kiddies round her and she was telling them a parable.

'Hope I'm not disturbing you, Sally,' I said.

'No, I'll always have time for the earthly father,' she replied.

'In that case I hope you won't think that what I'm about to say is of no earthly interest.'

I was trying to strike an easy-going note but it wasn't easy. Sally isn't exactly an easy-going person these days. She tilted her head on one side, smiled at me serenely, and generally gave the impression that she was about to converse with the village idiot.

'Speak father,' she said.

'It's all this religion lark,' I said. 'I just can't help wondering if it isn't all getting a bit out of hand.'

'It's all *in* hand. It's in the hand of the Lord.'

'Yes, I'm sure it is, and I'm glad that you believe that. So many young people don't seem to believe in anything at all. At the same time I can't help wondering whether you might be missing out on something.'

'What could I be missing? I nothing lack if I am his.'

'I think you're missing out on fun.'

'What sort of fun?'

'Going to parties, getting a bit tipsy, listening to pop music, dressing up in strange clothes, you know, all the things that young people do.'

'All the things you describe are the works of the Devil. I'm disappointed you didn't know that. I'm disappointed too that you'd try to lead me into temptation.'

Kids! Sometimes it's like talking to the wall, or in Sally's case like talking to one of those people who arrive on your doorstep and ask if you've heard the 'Good News'.

'Would you do something for me Father?' she asked.

I try to be an obliging parent. I try not to deny my children anything, but she had a look on her face that told me she was going to suggest something that I almost certainly wasn't going to want to do.

'Try me,' I said.
'Will you repent?'
'What should I repent about?'
'Everything. Your shallow, empty, meaningless life.'
'Steady on. I rather resent the suggestion that my life's empty. It seems fairly full at the moment.'
'But that only shows how truly empty it is.'
She fell to her knees in prayer, 'Oh Lord, look down on Eric thy unworthy servant . . .'
'For God's sake stop it, Sally. You're causing a scene. All the children in the playground are staring. And stop being so holier than thou.'
'But I am holier than thou, and that's why I'm begging you to repent. My eternal salvation is assured but yours must be in severe doubt. I wouldn't like to think of my father roasting in hell.'
I was a touch vexed. Who did she think she was to tell her own father that he was bound for everlasting torment? I may be as big a sinner as anyone but I still think I'm entitled to a little respect from my own daughter.
'You're not too old to get a thick ear,' I said.
'If you want to hit me that's all right. I'll turn the other cheek.'
I'll bet she would have too. I'd had enough. I withdrew before I said something I might regret.
'God bless you!' she called after me.
I didn't reply. God has a lot to answer for in my book.

Come the evening I was feeling in need of cheering up. Being held hostage and nearly losing your sight, having your Joan Crawford book drawn on, your courtesy car strafed and your soul condescendingly prayed for, doesn't leave you in the best of spirits. I was ready to be taken out of myself, otherwise I'd never have let Kathleen talk me into going to the variety show at the local civic theatre. I had all sorts of good reasons for not wanting to go. I don't like crowds, especially when they're in the theatre. I don't like theatres. And I don't like variety shows. I think they're all much of a muchness. I'd have been happier staying at home and making our own entertainment, so long as it wasn't a truth game. But Kathleen was very keen and so we went. Just the two of us. Max and Sally couldn't be persuaded. I suppose some might have thought it romantic.

The show was called *Skegness Stars* but if this lot were the stars I'm glad I didn't have to watch the supporting cast. Perhaps I was overcritical but I really didn't see the joy in paying good money to see a tuneless matron in lurex singing 'I am Sixteen Going On Seventeen', nor some old derelict performing 'Wimoweh' on a xylophone, and certainly there was no joy of any kind in watching some so-called comedian regaling us with his observations about British Rail and double-glazing salesmen. In fact I'd probably have walked out at the interval if it hadn't been for Kathleen. She downed a couple of gin and tonics and was ready for the second half which featured, among others, a stage hypnotist.

I've never held strong views on hypnotism. I'm sure it can be very helpful in losing weight, gaining confidence, giving up smoking etc. Whether that means it makes for wholesome holiday entertainment when presented on the variety stage I doubted from the beginning.

I don't know if you've ever seen one of these chaps operate. They begin by getting a fairly large group of people onto the stage, do a few simple stunts with them, and in the course of this the hypnotist discovers which members of the group are going to make good subjects. Gradually the less suggestible ones are sent back to their seats, leaving the two or three most easily hypnotised people on stage to make complete fools of themselves.

The hypnotist was a short, trustworthy-looking sort of chap in a white dinner-jacket with a round, harmless face and an avuncular manner. He asked for volunteers. They were slow to come. I need hardly say that I had no intention of getting up, but as bad luck would have it we had aisle seats. I'd thought this was a good thing since it would make it easier to walk out. However, it also made it easy for the hypnotist's assistant to catch my eye as she wandered into the audience to round up likely candidates.

I fought like a lion but I didn't have a chance. The assistant was pulling me from one side and Kathleen was shoving me from the other, and it got to the point where it would have been even more embarrassing to keep fighting than it was to give in, so I went on stage. Kathleen came too. There was no keeping her off.

We stood awkwardly with a dozen or so other people and the hypnotist told us we were getting younger, and some of the group started behaving like children, then like babies. Then we were told we were in a trench in the First World War and several people got shell shock. Then we were cancan girls. I really couldn't see the entertainment value of it, but I was relieved that while the others, Kathleen included, cavorted about like people not right I remained completely my old unhypnotised self.

I got sent back to my seat sharpish and that should have been enjoyable, but, once there, I had to sit through the rest of this unedifying spectacle, a spectacle that included my own wife.

There was an eighteen-stone man who was told he was a Christmas fairy and he danced about with his magic wand. There was a tiny old lady who was transformed into a sergeant-major. There were lots of other things but I'm pleased to say I've forgotten most of them. Suffice it to say that I wasn't entertained. The audience of course lapped it up.

Then things took an ugly turn. The hypnotist had been gradually sending people back to their seats. There were now only three volunteers left on stage, the eighteen-stone man, a typist from Grantham and Kathleen. The hypnotist convinced them that the two women were wrestlers and that the man was the referee. Kathleen at once took the typist in a Boston Crab and refused to let go. The so-called referee then became entangled and they all wrestled around on the floor. Somebody might very easily have been hurt if the hypnotist hadn't snapped them out of it, though I doubt whether Kathleen would have been that somebody.

Obviously seeing Kathleen as an ideal subject, the hypnotist told her she was a strip-tease artist at the Crazy Horse in Paris. I jumped out of my seat and protested. Things had gone far enough. 'Let's put an end to this sorry spectacle!' I cried. For reasons I can't imagine this seemed to amuse the audience.

The hypnotist came to the edge of the stage and fixed me with a steely eye and told me I was six years old, and suddenly there I was six years old and alone in front of a full theatre with every member of the audience laughing at me. I did what any six-year-old would do. I started sobbing and crying for my Mum. I couldn't believe this. I didn't feel hypnotised and yet I was acting as though I was. To considerable applause I went on stage and gave Kathleen a big hug as though she was my mother, but, of course, she thought she was a stripper at the Crazy Horse and she wasn't having any of it.

'Isn't this your little baby boy?' the hypnotist asked her.

'I 'ave no leetle beby boy,' Kathleen said in a very passable French accent. 'I am Madame Kathleen.'

'And do you have a husband, Madame Kathleen?'

'An 'usband I 'ave. Quel wanker!'

She moved her hand in an obscene way and brought the house down. Personally I'd hoped never to hear that word on Kathleen's lips. And if I ever *did* have to hear it I'd certainly have hoped not to hear it used as a description of me, and certainly not to a motley crowd of two thousand holidaymakers.

'Madame Kathleen, I think it's time for your act.'

'Mummy!' I screamed.

The hypnotist then explained to the audience that Kathleen wasn't actually going to do a strip-tease. Instead she would do an imaginary strip and take off imaginary stockings, gloves and bra, leaving her own clothes firmly in place. However, he seemed not to have explained this to Kathleen. Some stripper music started and instantly, quicker than I'd ever have thought possible, she'd taken off her actual clothes and was strutting about the stage naked. It was lucky Kathleen was so trim and attractive.

I think it was obvious even to the yahoos in the audience that this wasn't supposed to happen and the audience went into a shocked silence, though they were scarcely more shocked than the hypnotist. He tried to snap Kathleen out of it but by now she was trying, with moderate success, to remove the clothes of the eighteen-stone man.

The curtain came down, with Kathleen, the eighteen-stone man, the typist from Grantham and the hypnotist behind it, but with me in front of it facing the audience. I find this next part very hard to credit but I then treated them to a rendition of 'On the Good Ship Lollipop' complete with tap-dance. I ended the act by explaining I had to go now because I needed a wee-wee.

I was led away by a stage-hand and taken to a dressing-room where the hypnotist brought me back to normal. Kathleen was there too, more or less clothed now, and she seemed to be arranging an assignation with the stage-hand.

'I love showbiz folk,' she explained.

Words can barely express the pain, humiliation and anger I felt. I was appalled that this sorry show could pass for entertainment.

'At least the groundlings will think they've had their money's worth,' I said bitterly to the hypnotist.

'Not true squire,' he said. 'When people go bonkers like you two did, the audience always thinks you must have been plants.'

It is after midnight now. Kathleen is in bed. She has several times implored me to come to bed and 'do my duty'. I've had to be very hard with her. I've said I'm ashamed of her behaviour and I can't bring myself to share the same sheets. This is as good an excuse as any.

Upsetting though my encounter with hypnotism has been, I can't help thinking that some good may yet come out of it. If we want to know more about ourselves and our loved ones then I think we can't ignore the subconscious. In Kathleen's subconscious she's a French stripper. In my subconscious I'm a six-year-old boy crying for his mother. A lesson learned there I think, even if it was a painful one.

The pain wasn't eased any after the show as we got into our car. A group of young louts who'd obviously been at the performance saw me, whooped with derisive laughter and shouted, among other things, 'Hey look, it's bloody Shirley Temple.'

I was too sensible to make a reply.

*

All of which brings me to the subject of death. I may not agree with everything that Sally says but she certainly sets me thinking. Usually I don't worry much about death. There are two reasons for that. One is that I've got quite enough on my plate worrying about life. Two, I think death probably isn't such a bad thing. I mean there's so much of it about, everybody has to go through it, it's perfectly natural and there's no getting out of it, so I tend to think it's probably for the best. And even if it isn't for the best you're probably better off believing that it is.

As for what happens after death, that's another story. Straight away let me say that I don't hold with reincarnation. I've never fancied that at all. I mean, if you've spent seventy-odd years living quite happily in South Yorkshire you're not much going to appreciate coming back as a Guatemalan peasant, are you? Much less as a goat or a beetle or whatever.

Then there's this Heaven and Hell business, which sounds sort of reasonable in some ways, but I have my doubts. As a system I think it leaves a lot to be desired. Heaven and Hell just strike me as a bit extreme.

Let's say you're just an ordinary chap, you've never done anyone any serious harm, but all the same you're guilty of being envious, lustful, slothful etc. Well, according to the rule book there's no two ways about it, you're headed for downstairs. And when you get there you'll no doubt run into Hitler and Lucrezia Borgia and Jack the Ripper, and I expect they'll ask you what you've done, and you'll have to say, 'I was slothful.' They're just going to laugh in your face! You're just not going to fit in. It's like sending people to a maximum security prison because they're a week late paying their television licence.

And Heaven's not going to be any better. You may have been a good, honest, Godly sort of bloke, but when you get to heaven you'll be keeping company with John the Baptist, Mary Magdalen and St Christopher and all that lot, and you're not going to feel any more at home there.

If I was designing the system I'd have lots of intermediate grades, Heaven at the top and that would be really wonderful, and Hell at the bottom, and that would be hell, and about fifteen stages in between. You'd find the level that suits you best and stay there for all eternity. I think my idea could save everybody a lot of grief in the long-run.

Then again there might not be anything. You might just die and that's it – nothing. I think I'd be prepared to settle for that. Obviously it wouldn't be as good as heaven proper, but when you consider some of the alternatives, in fact even when I contemplate another night with Kathleen, I think you could do a lot worse than oblivion.

Saturday

Discovered this morning that there isn't a single bookshop in the whole of Skegness that can sell me a large coffee-table volume featuring Joan Crawford.

Being sensitive to criticism I've given some thought to what my lovely daughter Sally said about worshipping graven images. Perhaps it's true that I'm a bit obsessive in my admiration of Joan. Perhaps, as Sally pointed out later, it isn't just coincidence that she shares the same initials as the Son of God. But however you cut it I just can't see that Joan is a false God. For me she's the real thing.

The bookshops were a pretty sorry bunch, and the assistants made the sullen youth look positively subservient. They were all out of stock or they'd never been *in* stock, or they didn't know *what* they stocked, or they'd never heard of Joan Crawford. At one point I was offered a book on Joan Collins as a substitute.

What sort of world is it where bookshops don't stock coffee-table volumes featuring Joan Crawford? Not my sort of world that's for sure.

Everyone seems to be obsessed with sex these days. Not only my trim and attractive wife but also the newspapers, the television, films, and even the personable young chap with the stutter. I had recently returned from my bookshop visit when he sought me out. We talked about this and that and suddenly, apropos of nothing at all he said, 'Do you ever worry about the size of your equipment?'

If we'd been living in a different age he might have been referring to the tools I keep in my garage but being the age it is he was referring to my organ of generation.

'No,' I said. 'It's not worth worrying about, is it?'

'You probably only say that b-because you're b-b-b-built like a stallion.'

'Well I've never had any complaints.'

'See what I mean.'

'But I've never had any unsolicited testimonials either. I'm just very average.'

'You can't have degrees of averageness. Nature's left me well b-b-b-below average.'

Frankly this conversation was a good deal more intimate than suited me. Discussing penile dimensions with almost complete strangers rather offends my sense of the social niceties. On the other hand the poor chap did seem to be genuinely troubled and it only seemed right to do what I could to pacify him.

'Lots of women say it's not the size that counts but what you do with it.'

'I b-b-b-bet they only say that if you've got a small one. If you've got a b-big one I b-bet they don't say that. If you've got a b-b-big one I b-b-bet they don't care what you do with the b-b-b-b-bugger.'

I wasn't in a position to debate that. In fact I thought he might have a point, but I wasn't going to get gloomy about it, and I didn't want him to get any gloomier than he already was.

'You know that song by B-Burt B-B-Bacharach, "What the World Needs Now is Love Sweet Love", well what I think the world needs is cocks b-b-big cocks,' and then he started to sing, '"No not just f-for some, b-b-but for everyone".'

'Look,' I said. 'Those of us with average dimensions are very grateful to smaller chaps.'

'Why's that then?'

'Because,' I explained, 'if there weren't any small men then the average size would be statistically higher. If it weren't for small men the average would shoot up, then all the men who are currently average would be suddenly *below* average.'

I can't say that cheered him up very much. In the end he said, 'Mind you, when you've got a stutter it doesn't matter what size your equipment is. Even if you had a nob like a b-b-barber's pole, still nobody'd let you b-b-b-b-bonk 'em.'

'You've just got to do your best with what you've got,' I told him, not for the first time.

'If it wasn't f-for this stutter I could have b-been a b-b-bloody sex God.'

'If I were you I'd settle for being a bingo caller.'

This was meant to be bitterly ironic, and show him the foolishness of his misguided ambitions, but he wasn't a great spotter of ironies.

'All right,' he said. 'You've convinced me! I'll go f-for it! I'll b-become the b-b-best b-b-b-bingo caller in B-B-B-B-B-Britain!'

Why do people only hear the advice they want to hear? Why do so few people appreciate irony?

Given that Kathleen and I are both keeping journals I suppose it shouldn't have come as a surprise to find that Sally was at it as well. I came across her effort quite by chance as I was rooting through her suitcase looking for my sunglasses. The journal is in the form of a scroll and is headed *My Spiritual Diary*. I had quite a debate with myself about whether or not I should read it, but I *did* read it on the grounds that it could only help me to understand Sally that little bit better. Frankly it's slightly turgid stuff and rather 'samey', but I've copied out a representative passage, which, if nothing else, should be of interest as a case history.

My Spiritual Diary
FRIDAY

Woke up this morning. Saluted the new day. Was glad to be alive. Rejoiced in the world and all its bounty. Gave thanks for the many blessings that are bestowed on me today and every day. Thanked the Lord for my health and strength, wit, intelligence, insight, intuition and spirituality. Also for my considerable beauty, and for my superiority to so many of His other children.

Spared many a thought for those less fortunate than myself. Felt genuinely sorry for those who don't have my many blessings and advantages, gifts and talents;

those poor, sad, ordinary people who don't have the joy of knowing they've been chosen by God.

Lots of people say that the way to Salvation is a steep and rugged path, with many hesitations and falterings. Often the pilgrim is supposed to be beset by false starts, chooses the wrong fork, goes many, many miles out of his way before finding the true road. Can't agree. Hate to argue but I don't see the difficulty at all. The way is clear and well signposted, though perhaps not everybody has my impeccable sense of direction.

You hear so much about spiritual struggles and long, dark nights of the soul. Think I did the right thing by giving all that a miss.

Well aware that grace isn't bestowed on just anyone. Only given to a few supremely fortunate souls – mystics, saints – my kind of people. And all heaven and earth rejoices in our existence. Think I've done very nicely for myself.

Such a song and dance made about God being mysterious, elusive and unknowable. Well, he's not going to elude me.

When the fire of divine love takes hold of the soul it cleanses it of all sin and vice. My soul feels absolutely spring-cleaned.

Suppose I'm just lucky. Would consider myself luckier if I were in a first-class holy place rather than this dump the Tralee, but you can't have everything, at least not straight away.

Sometimes look at my humble origins and am amazed. Well-meaning but slatternly mother, dull father steeped in sin, poor useless brother. How does such unpromising and infertile ground bring forth *moi*?

Worry about father sometimes. I try to show pity and daughterly concern but not sure if he merits my serious attention. Sometimes think he's too far down the road to damnation to be bothered with.

Shall certainly try to remember him in my prayers but so much else to pray for that if by some chance he gets forgotten he'll just have to fend for himself.

Dear Lord, please help me to improve myself day by day. Think I'm doing amazingly well under my own steam but with you helping as well, how can I go wrong? Amen

They say eavesdroppers never hear good of themselves, and no doubt people who read other people's spiritual diaries are in much the same boat. Nevertheless, I do object to being called 'steeped in sin', especially when she can call her mother well-meaning. Is she trying to imply that I don't mean well?

Actually, as I read Sally's diary, I didn't feel very well-meaning at all, but I resolved to *be* well-meaning just to prove her wrong.

Was involved in a car chase today – another first. Kathleen and I left the kids to their own devices and went for a quick lunchtime drink. I had my usual bottled lager while Kathleen had something called a Maiden's Prayer. I'm a great stickler for finding the right pub and I didn't at all like the one that we went to, but Kathleen insisted. I think she only liked it because of the name: the Pump Inn.

We were sitting in the beer-garden, minding our own business when I noticed a car drive into the car-park. It looked just like mine. In fact the moment I saw it I knew it *was* mine, and it had been repaired. This was confirmed when I saw the driver; the Latin looks, the sleek hair of so-called Honest Iago. I thought I'd better have a quick word with him. I dashed across the beer-garden and waylaid him as he was opening his car door.

'Am I glad to see you,' I said. 'The car looks fine. I'll settle up with you now and you can have your old Wartburg back. Sorry about the bullet holes.'

A quick reply was not forthcoming. After a long silence he said, 'Do I know you, flower?'

'You most certainly do. And I know my car. I must say I think it was fairly disreputable of you to do a moonlight flit like that, but give me my car back and we'll say no more about it.'

He looked at me blankly for a while before saying, 'Who *are* you? Am I supposed to know what you're talking about? This is *my* car.'

'Is it? Is it indeed?'

He looked as though he was thinking again. Kathleen shouted, 'Be assertive' from the beer-garden. I could see that she'd invited a group of building workers to sit at our table and that threatened to be a problem in itself, but for now I could only worry about Honest Iago.

'You do know me,' I insisted. 'And you know that this is my car. You lent me a courtesy car, which incidentally the police seem very interested in.'

'Police?'

'Yes. Chief Inspector Hollerenshaw.'

'Hollerenshaw,' he said slowly as a look of blind panic swam across his face. 'Not Hollerenshaw. Anything but Hollerenshaw. Okay. You win.'

He slammed the door of the car, started the engine and began to drive off. That wasn't what I called winning. I shouted a bit and waved my arms but that really didn't delay him very much. That's when the car chase started. I chased him for a hundred yards or so, but it wasn't much of a contest since I was on foot. I thought of leaping in the Wartburg and haring after him, but by the time I'd have got it started and out of its parking space he'd have been miles away.

I stood forlornly in the car-park and I really did think I might have made a mistake in taking my car to Honest Iago; but then I saw the car returning. Could it be he'd seen the light? Might my words have pricked his conscience and made him decide to live up to his name? He drew into the car-park, wound down his window and looked at me.

'I've been thinking, flower,' he said.

'Good.'

'I've been thinking I shouldn't let some hamster like you make me leave the pub I want to drink at. I go where I want to go. I drink where I want to drink.'

That was the longest bit of continuous speech I'd ever had from him, but I didn't have much time to contemplate what he'd said because he then revved his engine and ran me down. It wasn't terribly serious as road accidents go, but it was a shock to the system and I have to say that the fact it was my own car that ran me down did rub salt into the wound. As did the fact that a van full of building workers was leaving the pub car-park the very moment it happened. They shouted a few ribald remarks at me, but I didn't bother to reply. As the van departed Kathleen was clearly visible through the back window, inside the van. She had a rather wanton look on her face, as did one of the builders who waved a lady's bra at me (if you can still call Kathleen a lady).

I picked myself up, dusted myself off, and returned to the table where I'd been enjoying my drink. The glass of lager was still there and I almost drank it, feeling in need of a little tipple. But I had to leave it untouched. What if one of the builders had spat in it?

I don't want to give the impression that I'm a drinking man but I do enjoy a leisurely bevvy when I'm on holiday. It helps me unwind, and I feel I still have a certain amount of unwinding to do before the holiday's over. So I bought myself a half-bottle of good whisky and took it back to the caravan all quiet anticipation. Sally was sitting on the sun-lounger and she turned to me rather pointedly and said, 'Drink is a mocker, father.'

'Thank you for sharing your views on the subject with me, Sally,' I said, perhaps a little harshly, and I hoped there would be no further discussions. Sometimes you're just not in the mood for being a caring father.

'Can I see the bottle?' she asked.

I saw no harm in it. At first I thought she was just reading the label very closely, but there was a strange glow in her eyes as though she was looking right through the bottle. Who knew what it was all about? Kids! Who'd have 'em?

'Finished?' I asked.

She didn't say anything, but she had a religious expression on her face and I took that to mean yes.

I pottered inside and poured a thimbleful of whisky into a glass. I was really looking forward to this. I was expecting to enjoy the fine bouquet, the rich taste, the golden warmth as the whisky played upon my tongue. Instead I got a mouthful of tepid, tasteless, coloured water.

'I've been sold a pup!' I exclaimed. I wondered if by some coincidence I'd been rooked by the same people who'd sold the Garcias their mescal with the worm in it.

My lovely daughter Sally was now standing in the doorway of the caravan, watching me and looking extremely smug.

'Jesus is all right by me,' she said. I didn't see what that had to do with my present problem but she continued, 'Yet I've always thought he'd have been doing the world a greater service if he'd turned wine into water instead of the other way round.'

'Are you trying to say . . .?'

'Yes father. I've just performed my first miracle. Aren't you proud of me?'

I thought about the price of whisky and I have to admit that I had mixed feelings. One of the reasons I needed it was for purely medicinal purposes. I still haven't been able to shake off this cold. I feel a lot less than 100 per cent and I'm now beset by back ache, occasional queasiness, and dry skin. But you try telling that to Sally.

Kathleen returned eventually. She looked flushed but content. I thought it best not to ask why. She went into the kitchenette and rustled up a fairly special turnip and corned beef *flambé*, so I didn't really feel I could complain.

After we'd eaten there was a knock on the caravan door and I opened it to see a very familiar face standing there.

'Terry,' I said. 'What are you doing here?'

Terry was my colleague from work, bright but without much chance of promotion. We'd sat in the same office for a couple of years now. He was an average worker, young and occasionally a bit cynical, but on balance a good man to have on the side I'd always thought. We'd shared many a small joke and he'd been there on that fateful occasion of the angst-ridden drink to celebrate my forty-fifth birthday.

'Found you at last,' he said.

'Did you lose me?'

'I'd never have found you at all if it hadn't been for your neighbours, the Garcias. They told me you were here. They seem like really nice people.'

'Looks can be deceptive Terry. Come in. The pot's still warm.'

'No,' he said. 'Let's go somewhere we can talk privately.'

It all seemed a bit odd to me, but I told Kathleen I was just popping out for a minute and we took a stroll by the river. I couldn't help noticing that Terry was dressed a little more flamboyantly than usual. He'd always been very sober at work, in a dark-blue suit and a plain tie. Now he was wearing an Hawaiian shirt and a pair of strawberry-coloured leather trousers. His hair had blond streaks and he was weighed down by a lot of jewellery. He was not the Terry I thought I knew, not that I ever thought I knew him very well.

'You're looking fit,' I said.

'I feel fit. In some ways I feel on top of the world, but I'm also feeling racked with guilt.'

'Guilt?'

'I feel guilty as hell actually.'

I invited him to tell me about it.

'The job's been really getting me down lately,' he said. 'I've been there two years, doing the bought ledger, getting pushed around by a lot of no-hopers (no offence), being forced to wear a suit, not having my worth recognised. Where was it all leading? What was the point of it all? I thought there had to be more to life.'

I'd never imagined that Terry would be an ally in my search for a richer existence. He'd always struck me as the kind of lad who was perfectly happy drinking a lot of rum and coke and sexually harassing the secretaries. I thought it showed how little we understand our fellow workers.

'So I made up my mind to leave. I decided a while ago but it really came to a head last Friday, the day before you set off on your holidays. I'd had enough. I didn't say anything to you because I didn't want to spoil your break. I decided to leave in a big way. I phoned the Chairman's wife and told her her husband was knocking off half the Xerox room. And I sent an abusive letter to the Managing Director in an envelope stuffed with used toilet paper.'

'I see,' I said. 'No wonder you feel guilty. It all sounds a bit immature, and very unpleasant.'

'I don't feel guilty because it was immature and unpleasant. I feel guilty because everybody thinks *you* did it.'

'Me? Why on earth would they think that?'

'Because I signed the abusive letter in your name. And on the phone I told the Chairman's wife I was you.'

'What?'

'Everybody at work thought it made sense. You've not been yourself lately. They all said it was because you're forty-five and are probably having a mid-life crisis.'

'I don't understand. Why have you done this to me?'

'I suppose because I'm a desperately incomplete person. Don't be too hard on me.'

'Hard? Hard? I can't believe this.'

'You'd better believe it Eric. But you see it's fortunate in a way. If they thought I'd done it, me, a nobody, a junior, then they'd have called in the security, the police, there'd have been hell to pay. Since they think you did it, and since you're so highly respected and have been there so many years, they're prepared not to press charges just so long as you never show your face at work again.'

'But this is crazy, Terry. Surely all I have to do is go along and explain everything. It'll be my word against yours, and as you so rightly say I'm very highly respected.'

'I'm highly respected too, these days,' he said. 'Since they offered me your old job. It was such a good promotion I decided not to leave after all.'

'I still think they'd listen to me.'

'But you'd also have to explain how it was that Sheila saw you writing the letter and overheard you making the phone call.'

'She did no such thing.'

'She says she did.'

'Little Sheila? Why would she say a thing like that?'

'Possibly because I slipped her a few quid. And you'd also

have to explain the shortages in petty cash and the pro-terrorist literature they found in your desk.'

'I suppose you put them there.'

'Hey, don't get angry Eric.'

'Get out of my sight before I set my boy Max onto you.'

'As a matter of fact I'd better be going. Your neighbours have invited me round for a drink. But before I go I'd like you to know how much better I feel for having told someone all this and got it off my chest.'

I've decided not to tell Kathleen and the kids about this trouble at work. I don't want to worry them. Not that much worries Max these days, except the elemental forces of nature; and now that Sally thinks she's found salvation nothing worries her at all. I think Kathleen still has a capacity for worry, but I suspect it's more likely to be about where her next climax is coming from, rather than about her husband's ruined career.

I've tried to stay calm. I am an intelligent man with lots to offer. Possibly I was stuck in a rut. Probably the time was right for a change of job. I'm not proud and I'm not afraid of hard work. I have lots of experience and I get on well with my colleagues.

On the other hand, I'm forty-five. I don't know anything except bought ledger and I won't get a reference from my last job, a job I've had for the last twenty-eight years. Let's face it, I'm worried sick.

It is now well after midnight, nearly two o'clock in fact, and I'm more than ready for bed. However, I'm delayed by two things; one a nose-bleed, the other what can only be described as raucous jungle music emanating from the Garcias' caravan. These things are not unconnected.

The so-called music, interspersed with Hispanic whoops and gunshots, had been going on all evening, quite spoiling my concentration as I tried to write my journal. I didn't want to make a fuss but when midnight rolled around I thought I wasn't being unreasonable in going over and asking them to turn it down. The idea that Terry might be in there as well only made it worse.

I pounded on the door for a while but answer came there none. Probably they couldn't hear me for the music. I'd have hurt my fist if I'd knocked any louder so I got my cricket bat and used that to beat loudly on the door. Even that wouldn't have worked but, as misfortune would have it, my palms were sweaty and the bat slipped, inadvertently punching a hole through the window in the door.

The music stopped. The door opened a tiny amount and Mr Garcia showed his large, bullish face.

'Eh gringo, what's the deal?'

'I'm sorry about that,' I said. 'I didn't mean to break your window.'

He shrugged. 'Okay then, I accept your apology.'

The door slammed shut and the music started again. I remained where I was, my circumstances scarcely improved. I knocked again with a similar lack of success. I pondered for a while but saw no way of attracting attention except by breaking another window. This, with great reluctance, I did. The music stopped. The door was thrown open and Mr Garcia reappeared. He was wearing only a pair of Bermuda shorts and rubber gloves. He was angry.

'You crazy, man?'

'I'm most certainly not crazy, I want to talk.'

'You want talk. I give you talk.'

He popped back into his caravan and emerged waving an American baseball bat.

'Maybe you want play ball.'

'No. I told you. I just want to talk. About the music.'

'Is after midnight. Some crazy gringo smashes my windows and says he wants to discuss music. Hey why don't we discuss counterpoint, violin technique, the art of the fugue? You on something man?'

'I'm not on anything except my high horse,' I said patiently. 'Look, I know you come from an alien culture where things are done differently, but in this country civilised people turn their music off at midnight.'

'You saying I'm not civilised?'

'I think you're deliberately trying to start an argument.'

'Hey, you smart kid.'

I didn't really see where we could go from here. Two grown men waving items of sporting equipment at each other in the middle of the night seemed no way to spend a holiday.

'Go to bed, you drunken oaf,' I said at last. 'We'll discuss this again when you're in a fit state.'

I've always had a way with words and I think that barbed remark must really have hit home. Otherwise I'm sure he wouldn't have jabbed me in the nose with the end of his baseball bat. The coward then went in, slammed his door and turned on the music again.

That is why I'm sitting here with right on my side, with blood on my face and with sleep a long way off. The music hasn't relented. In fact, since two windows of the Garcias' caravan are broken, it now sounds louder than ever. 'Tijuana Taxi' has never been one of my favourite tunes but I suspect I may have to get used to it.

Sunday

I was sitting on the sun-lounger. I was nursing my nose and reading, I'm slightly ashamed to say, a tabloid containing a scandalous piece about an estate agent who was also a cat-burglar, when the tabloid *caught fire*.

I was amazed. I've heard of spontaneous combustion but I'd never expected to be on the receiving end of it. Then I realised that standing beside me was a steely-grey character I'd encountered before, although on the two previous occasions he hadn't been holding a cigarette lighter.

'Hollerenshaw,' I said.

'Chief Inspector Hollerenshaw to you.'

'Why did you set my paper on fire?'

'To get a bit of attention and respect.'

'You may have got my attention,' I said, 'but respect is another matter.'

'Anyway, it's a free country. This isn't Russia you know. A man can set fire to another man's newspaper without having the KGB called in, can't he?'

I could see he was having a bad day and I really didn't want to make it any worse for him by attempting to argue.

I said, 'Can I help you with your enquiries, sir?'

'I'll give you "sir".'

'Sorry.'

Then he mellowed. 'You can as a matter of fact. I've got a few questions that I need answers to.'

'Fire away.'

'What kind of animal do I remind you of?'

'What?' I said in disbelief.

'I'll give you "what". You'll answer my questions and like it. This is a serious clinical test designed to locate your complete psychological profile. Follow? So what kind of animal do I remind you of?'

'A dog,' I said. I thought I'd try to humour him.

'What kind of dog?'

'Bulldog?' I offered dubiously.

'No need to be dubious about it. In this kind of test there isn't a right and wrong answer. What kind of tree do I remind you of?'

'An oak.'

'What kind of vegetable?'

'You don't remind me of a vegetable.'

'Good. Good answer. You sure you haven't done this sort of thing before?'

'I'm sure.'

'What kind of musical instrument?'

'A grand piano.'

'Are you sure about that? Don't I perhaps remind you of a French horn?'

'No,' I said, 'not at all. Why?'

'No particular reason. I was just trying out one of my pet theories. What kind of car?'

'An estate car.'

'But what make?'

'A Ford.'

'I'll give you "Ford".' His eyes lit up like a gas-fire. 'I'd advise you to think again on that one.'

'Oh, a Rolls-Royce,' I answered quickly, leaving aside the fact that Rolls-Royce don't make estate cars.

'I knew we'd get there in the end. Now where's that wife of yours?'

'She's in the caravan.'

He motioned for me to follow him in. I was glad that Max and Sally were elsewhere. I think young people should be protected from the likes of Hollerenshaw. Kathleen was on the bed wearing figure-hugging jeans and a boob-tube. She was painting her toe-nails a rather indecent shade of mauve.

'Off with your clothes wench,' Hollerenshaw snapped.

'Now really!' I protested.

'It's all right Eric,' said Kathleen. 'I'm always more than happy to co-operate with the police.'

Kathleen took her clothes off. I had the unhappy feeling that she might be getting a taste for it. Hollerenshaw looked at her with more than just professional interest.

'I'll take a few photographs for future reference,' he said.

He pulled out a miniature camera. As he snapped, Kathleen adopted a number of poses that would once have shocked me. If nothing else, I've become a good deal less shockable in the course of this holiday.

'Look Hollerenshaw,' I said, 'what on earth does this have to do with police business?'

'I might have expected that,' he said. 'Yes, you're just like all the rest, aren't you? The public seems to think that if you're not kicking down doors or giving villains the brass-knuckle treatment then you're not involved in proper police work. Let me tell you, today's policeman is very different from the traditional local bobby. Today he's a technocrat, a sociologist, a lateral thinker. Or like me, a student of the human psyche. But do we get any thanks for it? Do we get any praise or kudos? Do we hell.'

'I'm sure it's a hard life,' I said. 'If you've finished with me I'll go to buy myself another Sunday paper.'

'You're not going anywhere until I've finished with you. All right darling, you can put your clothes on and leave us alone. You know how it is. Man talk.'

Kathleen reluctantly dressed and left.

'Now for some free association. I say a word, you say the first thing that comes into your head. Woman.'

'Mother,' I answered.

'Sex.'

'Exhaustion.'

'Money.'

'Old rope.'

'Neighbours.'

'Noisy.'

'Foreigners.'

I hesitated. A vortex of association swirled round in my head. 'Different,' I said at last.

'That was a very telling hesitation,' Hollerenshaw said. 'Tell me about the Garcias.'

'Tell you what?'

'Tell me everything. Your thoughts and impressions, your innermost feelings. Give vent to your prejudices.'

'I don't have any prejudices. The Garcias are drunken and loud and obnoxious and don't have any consideration for other people, but that's not prejudice. That's the truth. Anybody can see that. Well, anybody who's unfortunate enough to live in the caravan next to them.'

'Don't get clever.'

Then he put me in an arm-lock. It really was excruciating and it made it very difficult for me to concentrate on what he was saying, but the gist was more or less as follows.

'The Garcias are visitors to these shores,' he said, 'and it's our job to welcome them. We don't criticise them. We don't ask them to turn their music down. We don't break their windows with a cricket bat. Do we?'

'No we don't,' I said in response to a sudden twist of my arm.

'No we don't. England used to be the jewel in the world's crown, a haven of liberality and the rule of law. Now it's been taken over by spivs, bully-boys, Paki-bashers, people like you.'

I really had to protest at that. I like England as much as the next man. I'm all for liberality and the rule of law, and I'm no spiv or bully-boy and I've certainly never bashed a Paki. Hollerenshaw yanked my arm to stifle my protest.

He said, 'It's a short step from asking the Garcias to turn their music down to sending them off to concentration camps.'

'Oh come on!'

'I'll give you "oh come on". Listen, I'll let you into a secret. I have a dream, Eric. You can call me crazy but I want to build the new Albion. I wonder if you can help.'

He let go of my arm and produced a personal stereo from his suit pocket. It was one of those stereos that operates with two sets of headphones. He wrapped one pair round my ears and put the other on himself. 'Listen to this.' The tape started to play, and although I didn't know for sure I'd probably have guessed it was Mozart. The music was quite nice but not really to my taste.

'*Eine Kleine Nachtmusik*,' Hollerenshaw said. 'That boy Mozart, he was a genius.'

Then the waterworks started. Hollerenshaw sobbed uncontrollably. I offered him my hanky.

'You, me and Mozart – the new Albion. What do you say?'

I said sure, why not, let's form the new Albion, whatever that involved. It seemed to make him happy. He packed away his personal stereo and to my considerable relief appeared to be ready to leave. I know our police are overworked and I didn't want to add to the load. As he turned to go he kneed me, very effectively, in the genitals and from my position on the ground I heard him say, 'And if I find you stirring up any more racial hatred, you're a dead man.'

Life's funny, isn't it. There was Kathleen the other night revealing her dwarf fantasy and today two male dwarves have moved into a nearby caravan.

I went and did the neighbourly thing by introducing myself. They seem like nice chaps, and it appears they work in the entertainment field. I would probably have guessed that, even if they hadn't told me, by the fact that they were wearing blue, sequinned jumpsuits and did a variety of headstands and comic falls while I was trying to talk to them. No doubt they were perfecting their act.

They were civil enough, but not exactly warm and friendly. Perhaps they felt embarrassed by their tiny stature. I came right out and told them there was no need for them to be. Still, if they want to keep themselves to themselves that's their business, and considering Kathleen's fantasy it may be no bad thing.

The Tralee Carapark and Holiday Centre has mostly static pitches, but there are one or two available for caravanners who are passing through and only want to stay a night or two. The mobile caravanner is a different breed from we static types but they're none the less welcome because of that.

A caravan arrived today, the like of which I'd never seen before. It was huge and incredibly ornate. It was painted pink and had smoked-glass Georgian windows with shutters, lots of chrome all over it, some wood-panelling, murals and rows and rows of flashing lights. The tyres even had white walls. Basically it looked like a tart's bedroom; an impression that was confirmed by a small neon sign above the door which read, 'Texas model – orgasms while you wait.'

You won't catch me bad-mouthing prostitutes. It's an old profession and many of the girls no doubt have hearts of gold. Nevertheless, I think that if society were a happier and saner place there wouldn't be any need for prostitutes. And I think the men who are their customers are a fairly sick and sad bunch, and I think they ought to be helped, forcibly if necessary. But since society isn't happy and sane, and since nobody's helping these unfortunates, I suppose prostitution's here to stay. Whether it should be here to stay in the Tralee Carapark and Holiday Centre is another matter.

I decided to stroll over to this new caravan and have a quiet word with the owner and suggest that she, or possibly they, might like to move on to another, less select site where they'd no doubt be more welcome. I really couldn't see any of the clean-living types who frequent the Tralee having much use for a model, Texan or otherwise.

I knocked on the door in a firm but fair manner. A pleasant, slightly husky, possibly Texan, female voice invited me to cross the threshold. I did so.

It took my eyes a little while to get used to the lack of light. I was certainly impressed by the central heating, which verged on the tropical, and by the deep burgundy carpet that was lapping round my shoes. The place was every bit as impressive inside as out. There were lots of mirrors, crystal chandeliers, gold fittings throughout, even a padded bar. In the midst of all this opulence I could make out a curvaceous female, lolling rather provocatively on a black fur couch. I couldn't believe my eyes. It was a vision.

She was wearing a flimsy black dress, low-cut to show an ample but not excessive cleavage, and the dress was slit to the thigh to reveal one long, slim, tanned leg. The shoulders were bare, and a mane of red hair cascaded over them. She was sexy and statuesque. She had flashing eyes, a finely chiselled nose with flaring nostrils, and a warm, melting mouth. She was distinguished, determined, passionate, perhaps a little haughty. The exquisite creature before me was none other than the spitting image of Joan Crawford. My heart skipped several beats.

I suppose I should have been asking myself all sorts of questions about who, why and how; but I was too stunned and delighted to start demanding explanations.

'Can I do anything for you?' she asked.

Even the voice was a passable imitation of my icon.

'What *can't* you do for me?'

'That's right,' she said. 'I can do almost anything. I'm yours for the asking.'

This was unbelievable. It was a dream come true. More than that, a hundred dreams, a million. It was a real holiday highlight. Joan Crawford was as good as mine. (Obviously not the real Joan Crawford, I know she's been dead for more than ten years, and even if she was alive she'd be eighty plus, but Joan Crawford, near as damn it, was as good as mine.)

I don't know what came over me. I'm a married man. I love my wife and children. I'd die rather than hurt them, but in that one moment they counted for nothing. Security, marriage, family life, they could all have gone to the wall. It was madness.

I'm happy to say that I'm far from a practised seducer, but at that moment I felt like Don Juan. I was ready for anything. Even my debilitating nights with Kathleen didn't seem to be affecting me. My cold even seemed to have cleared up. I tore off my sports-shirt and sweater, my slacks, my shoes, my briefs, my wristwatch.

'Take me, I'm yours,' I said.

'Aren't you going to undress me?' she enquired.

'Of course. Of course. How rude of me not to have offered.'

My hands were shaking but I tackled the job. I slipped the dress from her beautiful shoulders. I undid the zip to reveal her long, smooth back. Her breasts were full. Her legs were stylish. Her waist was slender. Everything looked the way it should.

Perhaps I was a little neglectful on the foreplay, but I thought there'd be plenty of time for that later. Very rapidly my hands roved over her bosom, over her flat tummy, and down inside her skimpy silk knickers. There all was not as it should have been at all. I got the fright of my life.

What should have gone in actually came out. Where there should have been a valley there was a peak. Where there should have been a soft, yielding entrance to her secret self there was a bloody great willy. (Pardon my French.) I was stunned.

I know when I've been had. This Joan Crawford was a sham, a transvestite, a hermaphrodite, the kind of thing you read about in the tabloids. Call it what you like, I didn't want any part of it. I was horrified. My dreams were in rags.

I wanted to run from that place, screaming, gagging, and wailing with anguish. However, that would have meant running round the Tralee in the nude. So, with all the dignity I could muster, I put my clothes on and tried to make a tactical withdrawal.

'That'll be fifty notes,' the creature said.

'Oh no it won't!' I cried. 'If you think I'm paying for this you've got another think coming.'

It appears these transvestites can be very strong. Also a bit violent. He wrestled me to the ground and took all the money I had. It was less than the fifty pounds he was demanding but it still didn't feel like good value for money.

I couldn't leave without trying to salvage some snippet of self-respect. I held my head up and said sharply, 'There's one thing Joan Crawford had that you'll never have, and that's *class*.'

This being a Sunday, Sally was in a pretty funny mood all day. I came across her this afternoon wrapping bandages around her hands and feet. Naturally I made fatherly enquiries to see if it was anything serious.

'Stigmata,' she said.

'Oh,' I said, not wanting to show my ignorance.

I've never heard of it but I guess it must be one of those women's ailments that a gentleman doesn't delve too deeply into. The inner workings of the female body have never been an open book to me, and frankly I think I prefer it that way.

Was mugged again this evening. I'm afraid this is becoming an all too regular occurrence in the Tralee Carapark and Holiday Centre. Since the Joan Crawford look-alike had taken all my money I'd just been into Skegness to find a cash dispenser. I came back reasonably flush with cash. I had a smoke in the toilet block and was returning to my caravan when I was set upon by two lads in track suits. They grabbed me from behind and went through my pockets. Since I was carrying plenty of money I thought they ought to be happy and therefore unlikely to beat me up. But no. They beat me up anyway.

As I lay on the ground I shouted defiantly, 'I suppose you enjoy beating up quiet, unassuming forty-five-year-olds who don't defend themselves.'

'No,' they said. 'We just enjoy beating up *you*.'

Yes, there are some advantages in being quiet and unassuming and not defending yourself, but at the moment it's hard to see what they are. The meek may inherit the earth, but in the meantime it's a bit like sitting around waiting for an aged relative to die. There must be another way.

I have come to the conclusion that what this country needs is some Militant Niceguys. They'd be a secret organisation and the members would appear to be very ordinary men in the street, quiet, unassuming, with responsible, if mundane, jobs, but when their moment came they'd be brave and fearless as lions.

Let's say a Militant Niceguy was walking down the street and came across some oik dropping litter. The Militant Niceguy would go over and reason with him. If reasoning did no good he'd employ highly developed self-defence techniques and knock the offender to the ground. 'That's right,' he'd say calmly. 'Get down on the ground where you belong, with all the other rubbish.'

If the Militant Niceguy found someone smoking in a no-smoking area he'd begin by taunting the miscreant. 'Is it that you can't read, or is it that you're a pathetic, antisocial little yob?' Then he'd discharge a small fire-extinguisher over the villain, a specially designed portable extinguisher that he'd carry at all times for just such an occasion.

If one of the Militant Niceguys were mugged he would thrash his assailants to within an inch of their lives, using a combination of subtle eastern arts and good old Queensberry Rules.

The Militant Niceguys would deal with people who talk and rattle their crisp bags in the cinema. They'd sort out people who throw up in the street, who slam their car doors, who let their children run wild in public places, who jump queues, who don't pay their library fines, who don't wash out their milk bottles and return them every day. That sort of people.

But will it happen? Will we see such a fine body of men walking the streets of this land? I don't know. Somehow I doubt it. I'd love to be one of them. I'd even like to be their founder and leader, but let's face it, you know how it is with niceguys – they just don't have any oomph. I'll no more become a Militant Niceguy than the personable young chap with the stutter will become a bingo caller. Still, it's good to dream.

Well, I say it's good to dream. Given the present state of my subconscious I'm not so sure that it is. Some of my most recent dreams have featured falling into a bottomless pit, being eaten by a black widow spider, sinking into quicksand, and being trapped by a landslide in a railway tunnel.

However, I do at least have some hopes that tonight I'll get a good eight hours sleep. Earlier in the evening I ground up some sleeping-pills that we happened to have lying around and put them in Kathleen's bedtime drink (a couple of cans of extra strong lager).

I realise that this isn't exactly the most chivalrous act a loving husband ever performed, but Kathleen is no damsel in distress, and even Sir Lancelot himself would be getting a bit desperate if he had to live with what I've been through. And so, full of hopes of oblivion, to bed.

Monday

I always knew it was wrong to put any faith in drugs. The sleeping-pills had no effect. If anything, Kathleen was livelier than ever. And when I wasn't pandering to Kathleen, in those few brief moments when she let me fall asleep, I kept having terrible nightmares about having been sold into white slavery by Joan Crawford and having to service the needs of a boat-load of female pirates.

I was glad to see the sun come up.

Set off on my morning constitutional and before long I fell in step with the old chap with the radical views. We chatted happily enough but I admit I was wary. I didn't want the conversation to slip into those areas that made the old guy demented. So we skirted round a number of issues; proportional representation, dandruff, Louis Pasteur, and the dangers of unguarded fires. All seemed to be going well and perhaps my guard was down, but we began to talk about those women who stand around in supermarkets and try to get you to sample new food products. You'd have thought it was an innocent enough topic but suddenly the old boy was transformed and he was off again.

'Do you know what I'd do with those women who stand around in supermarkets and try to get you to sample new food products? I'd round them all up and lock them in football stadiums and make them commit sex acts with animals while their families watched. That'd show 'em.'

'You're not wrong there,' I said.

'Of course I'm not.'

'You can say that again.'

Now that I was agreeing with him he was all smiles. He seemed as nice an old gent as you could possibly wish to meet.

'But there's one thing that bothers me,' I said, and I knew I might be taking my life in my hands here. 'How come you're so in favour of doing all these terrible things to people, yet you didn't have enough gumption to no-ball Max? I know you said you were scared of him, but some of these women in supermarkets are fairly fearsome as well. They're not going to just stand there and let you do it, are they?'

'There's a simple explanation,' he said.

I'd had a feeling there might be.

'I'm like Karl Marx in that respect,' he said. 'Marx wasn't some bomb-throwing revolutionary. He was a philosopher, a thinker. I'm the same. I'm just a theoretician. The practitioners come later.'

Well, it seems not to have been just a trick of the light – the headless corpse I mean. I was returning from the shower block when I passed a caravan that appeared empty yet had its door wide open. I'm a stickler for security, so, at the very least, I thought I'd be a good neighbour and shut the door for them. However, the door handle had got something unpleasant on it and there was what looked very much like human entrails all over the doorstep. I suspected something was up. I stepped inside, had a squint around, and couldn't help noticing that someone had smeared '666' on the wall in blood, and that there was a headless corpse lying by the cooker.

This seemed more than just coincidence. A headless corpse in the hospital, a headless corpse in the fog, and now one in a caravan. They say bad luck always goes in threes. It was enough to convince me that something funny is going on around here.

I suppose to be absolutely correct I should have reported the incident to the police, but frankly I didn't want to get involved. I particularly didn't want to get involved with Hollerenshaw again. Basically I didn't want anything else spoiling my holiday. If you ask me this world would be a much better place if people didn't interfere in other people's business.

I was raped today, and it really is every bit as bad as everyone makes out. It left me feeling unclean. As I write I'm feeling humiliated and disgusted; and I'm sure they're right when they say that rape is a crime of violence and power, not of sex.

It started innocently enough when Kathleen suggested that we return to the Pump Inn. I was a bit reluctant after my last experience there, and I was afraid that Kathleen might only want to go in order that she could meet up with the builders again. Anyway, I still can't deny that woman anything so we went to the Pump Inn. We sat in the beer-garden again and I enjoyed a bottled lager while Kathleen drank something called a Killer Zombie. All seemed right with the world. I should have known it couldn't last.

I'd been vaguely aware of a slightly odd-looking pair of Girl Guides who were sitting in a corner of the garden. They were drinking spirits and chain-smoking. It didn't exactly seem to fit with the ideals of the Girl Guides as I know them, but I supposed they'd somehow lost their troop, and like so many young people were taking the opportunity of being away from supervision to taste a few forbidden pleasures. When will they ever learn? However, they did look very accustomed to drinking and smoking, and as I looked more closely at them they certainly appeared a bit long in the tooth to be Girl Guides.

I tried not to stare, but I thought I'd better keep an eye on them. Every time I looked in their direction they were looking back at me, and before long they started winking at me, giving me the eye, running their tongues round their lips in a lascivious manner, and in the end even waving at me. I tried to ignore it but it wasn't easy. I'm not used to being stared at by girls in uniform.

'What are you bothered about?' Kathleen asked. 'Most men would die to have a couple of Girl Guides giving them the eye. Think yourself lucky.'

I couldn't see that luck had anything to do with it. I became increasingly uneasy, and eventually had to suggest to Kathleen that we leave.

'That's not like you,' Kathleen said. 'Why should we leave? We've as much right to be here as they have.'

'That's true.'

'Why don't you go over and have a word with them?'

I knew she was right. A man of my age should be able to sit in a beer-garden without being sexually harassed. I also felt sure that a gentle word in the right direction would put a stop to their antics. All these types of people need is a firm word from a figure of authority and they soon start behaving themselves.

I eased myself across to the corner of the beer-garden where they were sitting. They giggled in a girlish manner as I approached. Once I got close to them they looked even less girlish than they had from across the garden. One of them was thirty-five if she was a day.

'Excuse me, young ladies . . .'

'We're so glad you came over,' one of them bubbled. 'We need a big strong man to help us with our tandem.'

So that was it. I might have known. They were using their so-called feminine charm in order to lure some man into doing a bit of bicycle repair for them. It was the old story. Surely, I thought, relations between the sexes haven't become as bad as that, have they? Surely a girl can ask a man to repair her bike without sex having to rear its ugly head. I was only too happy to be of service.

'All you had to do was ask,' I said. 'What's wrong with the tandem?'

'We're not mechanically minded. We don't know. It could be the chain or the inner tube, something like that.'

'Sounds like I'd better see for myself. Where's the machine?'

'Oh, over there,' and they gestured vaguely into the distance. 'We'll show you.'

We seemed to walk for miles. They were nice enough girls. They chatted happily and laughed a lot. We finished up by the river, nowhere near a path, in some very long grass. I couldn't imagine what anybody would be doing there with a tandem.

'Much further?' I asked.

'All the way,' one of them said.

She laughed heartily. Then she took off her uniform. I was amazed. The body that was revealed was not that of a Girl Guide. Nor did her underwear look like regulation issue. It was a good deal too black and flimsy for that, and it immediately aroused my suspicions.

'I know it's a warm day,' I said, 'but I'll thank you to cover yourself up.'

I turned to her friend and she too had peeled off her clothes to reveal similarly inappropriate undies. Something was very amiss.

'All right,' I said. 'If you two want to sunbathe I'll leave you to it. Just point me at the tandem and I'll do my best.'

'There isn't any tandem, silly.'

Curse it! A trap! I should have known. I panicked. I tried to run but the two harpies took hold of me and pinned me to the ground. I like to think I fought with the strength of ten men, but it wasn't enough, and in no time they'd stripped me naked and were doing all sorts of terrible things to me. Actually they were very much the same sorts of things that Kathleen has been doing to me, so there was nothing new about it, but that didn't make it any less terrible. I suppose as rapes go it could have been a lot worse, but this was certainly bad enough. You read about this sort of thing in books. You never think it'll happen to you.

Everything seemed to happen in slow motion. It was excruciating. A nightmare. What kind of world have we produced where this kind of thing can happen? Where were the police when I needed them? Where, for that matter, was Kathleen?

Kathleen, as I soon discovered, was standing ten feet away taking photographs. I looked at her pleadingly and uncomprehending. I couldn't shout to her because one of the Girl Guides was sitting on my face, but I think my eyes spoke volumes. Kathleen, however, was not lost for words.

'You look like you're enjoying yourself,' she said. 'I knew you would. You've been looking so down in the mouth lately I thought I'd do something to cheer you up. So I hired these two Girl-Guide-A-Grams. Don't say I never give you anything. Think of it as a belated forty-fifth birthday present.'

She looked extremely pleased with herself and took another photograph. I trust the lab will refuse to print it. The body sometimes has a mind of its own, and despite the horror and shame I was feeling I'm afraid my organ of generation rose to this sad occasion. As luck would have it, and thanks to the vigorous attentions of the women, it had soon done its sorry business. Fortunately that was the signal for them to end my ordeal. They tossed me aside like a used glove. I lay in the grass, my gorge rising, my tears flowing, while they dressed. Kathleen thanked them and handed over some money. I'm surprised she didn't give them thirty pieces of silver.

There was an ache in my body and soul as I dressed. Kathleen brushed me down. She was all smiles and wifely concern but that was just typical. I was almost speechless, but not quite.

'Kathleen,' I said, with all the restraint I could muster, 'just because your libido has become morbidly and perilously deranged, doesn't mean that *mine* has.'

'Well there's gratitude for you. I went to a lot of trouble to arrange this little treat, and this is all the thanks I get.'

'You expect thanks? You should be locked up!'

'I don't know what's wrong with you these days, Eric. You're just no fun anymore.'

'I never *was* any fun,' I said.

And just this once Kathleen let me have the last word.

News from home. A message was left at the site office asking me to ring my next-door neighbour urgently. My next-door neighbour is called Ken and is the sort of chap you could trust with your life, even if he is a bit slow returning the garden shears after he's borrowed them. Nevertheless, we aren't so pally that he'd ask me to ring him if there weren't some good reason.

'What's up, Ken?' I asked.

'You've been burgled,' he said. 'The buggers broke in last night.'

'Did they take much?'

'It's hard to say, but as far as I can see they didn't get away with anything at all. I think they must have been disturbed.'

'Probably they couldn't find anything worth stealing,' I said. 'Kathleen and I lead a simple life. We're not trammelled by video recorders or expensive jewellery.'

'I think that's right, Eric. And when they saw there wasn't anything worth nicking they smeared margarine all over your walls and corduroy settees, and went to the toilet all over your carpets.'

'Looks like we'd better come home at once.'

'No, don't do that. Why ruin your holiday? I'm here on the spot and I've got everything in hand. I've told the police, put new locks on the doors and windows, and if you like I'll get one of those professional carpet-cleaning people in to do the carpets for you.'

'That would be great. You're a prince, Ken.'

'I'm just doing what a good neighbour's supposed to do.'

Good neighbours – they're worth their weight in gold. I told Ken to keep up the good work, and with a chap like Ken you know you can rest easy. I've decided not to mention any of this to Kathleen. We aren't talking at the moment.

They say that to understand everything is to forgive everything, and I suspect that may well be true. I came on holiday hoping that I'd get to understand my kids better, but frankly it's been uphill work. I think I've had some moderate success with Sally. I now realise that she's some kind of pious, crazed, religious zealot. I may not agree with it but at least I understand it, and yes, I suppose I can forgive it; at least I'll be able to once she snaps out of it. Max, however, is a different matter. He remains incomprehensible and therefore unforgiven. In fact today, in trying to get to the bottom of things, I fear I may have made them worse.

My attempts at understanding him have been hampered by the fact that I never see him. He sets out every morning without so much as a packed lunch. He returns in the evening, late, by which time we've usually started the evening meal. He's dishevelled, covered in mud, and looks as though he's been in a fight with a wild animal. Sometimes he even returns with trophies from his expeditions: dead game-birds, rabbits, legs of beef. Certainly this cuts down on our butcher's bills, but lately he's been bringing home dead goats and badgers and they just haven't looked very appetising.

I suppose what pains me most about Max's unruly behaviour is that I feel essentially his heart's in the right place. Like me, he has a healthy dislike and distrust for many aspects of modern civilisation; he thinks it's empty, immoral and crassly materialistic. Who could disagree? But what can you do about it?

What Max has decided to do about it is smear his body with mud, let it dry to a sort of crisp outer coating, and wear a bone through his nose. At first I thought I'd say nothing about it, but then I thought no, if you don't take a stand that boy will never respect you and things will only get worse. Besides, he was dropping lumps of dried mud all over the caravan, so clearly something needed to be said.

I waited until he came home this evening. It was already starting to get dark. The rest of us had finished eating long ago. Max's meal was stone cold but at least we'd kept it for him, which in some ways was more than he deserved. He slumped at the table without first washing his hands, and messed his food around with his muddy fingers.

I wasn't quite sure where to start the discussion so I said cautiously, 'Exactly what kind of bone is that you've got through your nose?'

'Sheep. You want one?'

'No thanks.'

Max stood up, his nostrils twitching as if he was trying to pick up a scent.

'Please sit down, Max. I have an important question for you.'

Max grunted and sat.

'I'm not angry Max, I'm not even saying that I necessarily disapprove. All I'm asking is *why*? Why the bone? Why the mud? Tell me. I'll try to understand.'

'Because it's primitive. Because it's savage. Because body adornment is the first expression of man's creative impulses, and because it puts me in touch with the earth spirits.'

I think I'd have been well justified in asking just what precisely these earth spirits were and why he wanted to be in touch with them, but I didn't want to be hard on the lad, especially not when he was pouring out his heart.

'Look Max,' I continued, 'I'm not saying that you don't have a point, and certainly you're entitled to your own opinions, but I do feel that if you're going to continue to be part of this family then there are certain house rules that you'll have to start obeying.'

He glared at me with animal intensity.

'For instance, I think you ought to arrive a little more promptly for meals. I think you should make more of a contribution to family life. You should wash more often, help with cleaning the caravan, be a bit more sociable . . .'

Max let out a terrible roar.

'Don't you see Dad, this is all a sham.'

He gesticulated wildly at me, at Kathleen and Sally, at the caravan, at the world beyond. He picked up his plate, scooped the food into his mouth, licked the plate clean then threw it over his shoulder.

'If rejecting civilisation means an end to good table manners, then it seems a sorry show to me,' I said.

Max roared again. He knocked over the table, snatched up a chair and smashed it against the caravan wall. He started to leave.

'Just where do you think you're going, young man?'

After some more animal noises he said very distinctly, 'I'm going native.'

'In Lincolnshire?' I demanded, incredulous, but it was too late to argue with him. He was already out of the door and disappearing on all fours.

I suppose this wasn't exactly the effect I'd hoped my little chat would have, and if I had my time again I'd probably be more gentle with him, though frankly I'm still not sure exactly what I did wrong. Kathleen began talking to me again and accused me of being a bully and a home-wrecker, which I hotly denied. Nobody bullies Max these days. Basically I'm sure it will do Max the world of good to get away from the nest for a while, and, if nothing else, at least our little exchange has cleared the air.

To cap it all there was a storm this evening, the likes of which I've never seen. The day had been warm, not to say balmy, but as night fell a devilish wind got up, rain lashed the Tralee, and lightning tore the heavens apart. The caravan rocked on its base, while hail attacked the roof with a sound like gunfire. It was all extremely un-English.

It wasn't the night most people would have chosen for going native. I thought, briefly, of going out in search of Max, but I didn't. For one thing I didn't want to get soaked, for another I think it can only do Max good to have to take responsibility for his own actions and not expect his old Dad to come running to his aid. If nothing else it ought to make him appreciate the benefits of a nice, warm caravan.

In Max's absence I also came across his 'diary' for want of a better word. No doubt he's aware that Kathleen, Sally and I are keeping journals and he doesn't want to feel left out. Max has never been very good with words and I'm afraid it makes rather sorry reading. It is scratched on tree bark, written in some sort of dye. It mostly consists of rather messy doodles; drawings of arrow-heads, fish, ducks, snowflakes, wavy lines that might represent a river, an eye, an owl, a pair of walking legs. It all seems a bit rum. The only part of it that makes sense are the words 'The king must die' scratched across the bottom, though frankly that's not really my idea of sense.

It's after midnight now and I've been doing some fairly serious philosophising. I suppose really I've only been asking myself the same old questions I was asking myself back in the saloon-bar of the Devonshire Arms, but now I'm asking them with a certain extra desperation. Whereas before I'd have asked, 'What's it all about?' I now ask, 'What the bloody hell is it about, eh?' Whereas I'd once have said there might well be a more meaningful way of life, today I say, 'Surely, for the love of God, there has to be a better way than this doesn't there? Surely.'

I suppose it all comes down to a question of what a bloke ought to be doing with his life. I'm pretty certain that a bloke shouldn't be mugging people, or beating people up, or threatening them with ammonia, or stealing their car. But, on the other hand, what do I know? For all I know mugging people may be the way to revelation.

I mean, seriously, you see all these people in the world and somehow or other they don't seem to be troubled by the same day to day anguish that I do. How come? What have they got that I haven't? Maybe some of them have got faithful spouses and nice kids; and some of them probably even manage to have a pleasant, relaxing holiday once a year; and I'm sure all that helps but that doesn't seem to be the whole answer. I want to know what they really live for. Is it for spiritual advancement, the search for truth, for real values? Is it perhaps to help their fellow man?

Well no, don't be bloody daft, of course it isn't. What they live for is drink, television, new cars, fitted kitchens, dining-tables, etc. etc. It sounds a bit mindless to me but it seems to make them happy. Their lot certainly seems to make them happier than my lot makes me. And I'd be quite interested to know which of us is in the right.

Two things occur to me about this. One, suppose there's a Day of Reckoning, and then suppose that on that day you discover that all the sages and mystics were wrong, that it isn't spiritual values that count, only material values. What if you discover that it doesn't matter whether or not you lived a moral and virtuous life? What if morality and virtue don't count and all that matters is who had the biggest car or the poshest dinner-service?

Obviously it wouldn't be rational or fair. But since life never is, and never has been rational or fair, why should it suddenly become rational and fair on the Day of Reckoning?

The second thing that occurs to me is that there may not be a Day of Reckoning, in which case I don't suppose it matters a toss either way. If there isn't some final Day of Reckoning then the bloke who sells dodgy used washing-machines is the moral equal of Joan of Arc.

All these thoughts have been going through my head like clothes in a dodgy used washing-machine, and maybe I sound a bit gloomy and nihilistic; however, I think I may just have had an insight. A moment ago I put down my pen and looked across the caravan and saw a sign. The sign reads, 'Please leave this caravan in the state you would wish to find it.' If you widen the boundaries a bit then that sounds like a pretty good creed to live by. The only problem being that

I seem to be one of the very few people to take notice of such signs.

I've had enough philosophy for one night. I'm about to go to bed now. I'm no fool. I've given up all hope of keeping my trim and attractive wife either happy or quiet. Since sleeping-pills appear to have no effect on her I've been forced to consider even more desperate action. Tonight I shall be taking some sleeping-pills myself.

Tuesday

A pale dawn light filtered in through the curtains this morning. It was very early. I hadn't slept well. The pills did no good and I'd had a fairly unsavoury dream about being eaten by a vagina with teeth, and so I was awake to hear the sound of motorcycles entering the Tralee Carapark and Holiday Centre.

I opened the curtain to peer out. There must have been a dozen or so of them; big, old, British bikes, very solid, very noisy. The riders were a rough-and-ready lot. They were unshaven, unclean, and in most cases didn't have complete sets of teeth. Of course they were wearing scuffed black leather, with lots of zips and skulls and studs. They were all animal magnetism and brooding menace. I know you can't judge a book by looking at its cover, but these lads didn't seem to want you to get past their covers.

The Tralee is pretty strict in enforcing its 'no-motorcycle' policy, but there was nobody official around to tell them they weren't welcome. I thought it needed to be done before they got too settled in and since I was the man on the spot, I saw what my duty was. I'm not the sort of chap who likes to throw his weight around, but I find increasingly that you can't just let people do what they want.

I slipped on my socks and sandals, wrapped my dressing-gown around me, and went out to offer some friendly advice. The morning was chilly. Exhaust smoke blew around in big blue clouds. I gave the Hell's Angels a cheery wave but they didn't wave back. They were engrossed in their own activities, drinking beer, revving their engines, and shouting at each other, although I think they were probably only shouting because that was the best way to make themselves heard above the noise from the engines.

'Excuse me,' I said, but nobody seemed to hear me. It was just like the Garcias writ large. I excused myself again, louder this time, but it was hopeless. In the end I had to tap one of them on the shoulder.

I don't think he liked being tapped. No doubt that's why he pulled a knife on me, but I think he just did it for effect. I don't think he really intended to stab me, not then anyway.

One of the others clearly saw that pulling a knife was a bit unnecessarily hostile so he offered me a beer in friendship. I had to decline even though I wanted to be friendly. It was far too early in the day for me. But they didn't like having their hospitality turned down any more than they liked being tapped on the shoulder. I was seized roughly and held in position while the man who'd offered me the beer shook the can vigorously and opened it in such a way that a torrent of beer splashed all over me. I might have been prepared to laugh that off as youthful high spirits but it was no laughing matter when he grabbed my nose, forcing me to breathe through my mouth. He then filled my mouth with cold, beery froth. At least it was no laughing matter for me. The bikers seemed to think it was a hoot to see me choking and spluttering and trying to pass beer out of my nostrils.

Then they let me go. No doubt the average caravanner would have scuttled back to his bunk, but I'm afraid I'm made of sterner stuff. As it happened, I still had a mouthful of beer and I spat this mouthful out into one of their faces. It was probably a mistake. I understand these gangs have a pretty highly developed sense of what is and isn't permissible within their own codes, and I'd obviously overstepped the mark. They pulled my dressing-gown off, beat me with a chain once or twice, then knocked me to the ground where they forced me to lick their boots clean. This was a big job. They were big boots and they were fairly dirty, and I didn't like to think what the dirt consisted of. It was a grim experience and fairly hard on the tongue.

When I'd finished they picked me up, gagged me, tied me to a tree and started stubbing out cigarettes on my bare chest. It stung like nobody's business but I held my head up. I've never been the kind of man to kowtow to a group of smelly desperadoes, and even if you can't beat them I think you have a duty to suffer with dignity. I may have been powerless, but I stood firmly against the tree, my every muscle screaming defiance. Even my chest, which was starting to look like a badly abused pub table, was screaming defiance. I couldn't scream defiance with my mouth because of the oily rag they'd stuffed in it.

It's hard to say how things would have turned out if my lovely daughter Sally hadn't come running out to help her old Dad. Isn't it typical? A caravan site full of so-called men, and the only person who comes to your aid is a fifteen-year-old girl.

I must say Sally wasn't looking her best. She was wearing what looked like a sack, and it had ash marks all over it. She also had a wreath of thorns twisted round her head, which I thought was uncalled for. Nevertheless, she had a definite aura about her.

I really dreaded to think what these greasers might do when they saw Sally. However, the first thing they did was leave my chest alone, which was most welcome. But then they surrounded her. I feared things might get ugly. I thought they might force her to swallow beer, or worse. But no. She said, 'Peace be with you' and immediately the bikers went very quiet. She touched each of them in turn and blessed them. They seemed to enjoy that.

When I last saw Sally she was on the pillion of a Norton Commando, leading the pack of Hell's Angels out of the Tralee Carapark. It seemed no way for a young girl to be spending her holidays, yet I was pleased that her gentleness had achieved what my aggression couldn't. A lesson learned there, I thought.

Felt pretty groggy for the rest of the day. The cigarette burns were bad enough, but in addition to them I had a raging toothache, stomach cramps, muscular spasms, and a nasty taste in my mouth.

I'm not the sort of man to moan, but sometimes a good moan can put you right back on your feet. If nothing else, this journal is a good friend to moan to.

*

In the afternoon Kathleen and I had a saunter around the Skegness pleasure beach, and I was forced to ponder what we mean by pleasure, but that didn't take long and I amused myself by throwing darts and taking Kathleen on the Waltzer. It was nice enough but I'm not sure I'd describe any of it as pleasure. Kathleen did embarrass me slightly by asking the Waltzer attendant whether he had a pistol in his pocket. 'No,' the lad replied. 'It's an erection.' Fortunately I was able to spirit her away before too much damage was done.

As we passed a bingo stall I couldn't help noticing there was a bit of a riot going on. I looked more closely and saw that an ugly crowd of matronly women was threatening violence to a young man. They were furious, shouting and swearing and pulling at his clothes and hair.

'Let me go you v-v-v-v-vixens!' he shouted back.

Yes, it was none other than my constitutional companion, the personable young chap with the stutter. He was lifted head high by the women, who then threw him bodily out of the stall. He landed at our feet in a messy pile. His clothes were shredded, and blood had been drawn in several places. We helped him to his feet and asked what the problem was.

'I went f-for it,' he said, 'I asked them to give me a chance as a b-b-bingo caller and they did. It was great at f-first. I was all right on the two little ducks and legs-eleven and clickety-click and top of the shop. The problems started when I got two f-f-f-fat ladies, and all the f-f-f-fives, and on its own number f-f-four, and when f-f-fifty-f-f-f-four came up, closely f-followed by f-forty-f-f-f-f-five, I was f-f-f-f-finished.

'Nobody knew what I was trying to say. They got mad. They started shouting house before they had all their numbers, and when I came to check the numbers by reading them out again I had more of the same problem. And when I told them not to be such silly b-b-bitches they turned v-v-v-violent.'

I tried to be consoling but I didn't feel there was much I could say.

'I was a b-b-b-bloody f-fool,' he said.

'Don't blame yourself,' I said weakly.

'I don't, I b-b-blame you.'

The crowd of angry women had returned to their seats. The violence seemed to have gone out of them, but the stuttering chap ran over to them, and the mere sight of him seemed to infuriate them all over again. However, he had a great way of diverting their anger.

'It's his f-fault,' he said, pointing at me. 'He's the one whose b-b-b-big idea it all was.'

I thought that was a bit rich. I thought a chap should be responsible for his own actions. I also thought that whichever clown was gormless enough to give him the job on the bingo stall had something to answer for as well, but I didn't have much time to argue the matter. I ran, hotly pursued by the incensed female bingo crowd. I've heard it said that some women are beautiful when they're angry but I didn't notice it on this occasion. They caught me by the ghost-train. They thrashed me with umbrellas and handbags, and I had one of those windmills on a stick shoved in my groin. They pulled my hair, scratched me with their nails and trod on me with their low heels. I know some chaps are supposed to like that sort of thing, alas I'm not one of them. I curled into a ball, and once I'd stopped moving they left me alone.

I went to the car-park. Kathleen and the young chap were already in the Wartburg, both on the back seat. She was attending, with great concern, to his cuts and bruises. I'm not saying they didn't need attending to, but they definitely weren't as bad as mine.

I drove home. When we arrived Kathleen said, 'What you need is a nice relaxing massage,' but of course she wasn't talking to me. Kathleen and the stutterer disappeared into our caravan and I had to wait outside. He came out some considerable time later, and to be honest he didn't look any happier than he had when he'd gone in. I know that some animals are supposed to be sad after making love, but I didn't know the same thing applied after massage.

I know that a lot of people might find it a bit off for a wife to give a rub down to a more or less complete stranger on the very day that her daughter's gone off with a group of Hell's Angels, and only one day after her son's gone back to nature. All I can say is that I, too, am one of those people.

A phone message was left at the site office asking me to ring my parents. The message was from my old Dad. He's seventy-six and marvellous for his age. Mam is too. But when they get to that sort of age you can't help worrying once in a while. So, fearing the worst while hoping for the best, I rang home.
 'About time,' Dad said.
 'I rang as soon as I could. Is everything all right?'
 'Depends what you mean by "all right". Are you sitting down?'
 'No. I'm standing in a booth next to the burger bar, actually.'
 'Then I suppose that'll have to do. It's your Mam.'
 'Oh God. What's happened? Is she all right?'
 'Well, in a way.'
 'I don't understand.'
 'No. You always were a thick bastard, Eric. You see your Mam and me got talking last night.'
 'Good. It's great that you still have lots to say to each other after all these years.'
 'Shut it, Eric.'
 'I'm not a child you know.'
 'I know. You're a forty-five year old who's got no more sense than he was born with, so put a sock in it while I've told you my news. We were sat there, your Mam and me, watching *News at Ten* when suddenly she says to me, "You're not the natural father of our Eric".'
 'What?'
 'Naturally I thought she'd had one too many port and lemons, but no. It turns out your real Dad was an American sailor whom she met while I was away in the Med fighting against the Axis powers.'
 'I'll go to the foot of our stairs,' I said.
 'I thought you might say that.'
 'I'm fair gobsmacked.'
 I must admit I do tend to fall into these quaint dialect expressions when I'm talking to my Dad.
 'I thought you might be, but I thought you'd like to know.'

'Well of course, but what about you? What are you going to do?'

'I was thinking of making myself a toasted teacake.'

'You're taking all this very calmly,' I said.

'On the outside maybe, but inside I'm dying quietly, so I am.'

'I want you to know one thing, Dad. It doesn't make any difference to the way I feel about you. I still love you like a father. Nothing can ever change that.'

'You're a daft twat sometimes, Eric,' he said. 'It turns out that I've been living a lie, that my whole life's been a charade and a farce, and you say it doesn't make any difference. Are you cracked, or what?'

'But Dad . . .'

'I never want to hear that word pass from your lips again. In fact from this moment you're a stranger to me, Eric. I never want to see you or hear from you ever again. Understand?'

'But the grandchildren. Your pride and joy . . .'

'Somebody else's grandchildren. Somebody else's pride and joy.'

Then the phone went dead. I put the receiver down and left the booth feeling a bit stunned.

'Well,' Kathleen said, 'if you don't want to get tattooed, how about a bit of erotic piercing?'

'Pardon?' I said.

'A ring through the nipples, a bolt through the glans, that sort of thing.'

'If you must have a souvenir, I still don't see what's wrong with a trivet.'

I was hoping to make light of it. I didn't really want to discuss bodily mutilation with Kathleen at that moment. I had other things on my mind.

'You'd look a right berk with a trivet through your cock,' Kathleen snapped.

I hadn't come on holiday to hear language like that.

'You've been watching too much television, Mother,' I said.

She hates it when I call her 'Mother'. That's probably because she's not very motherly. That's probably why she isn't very distressed about the disappearance of Max and Sally. That's probably why I didn't tell her I'd been disowned by my father. She'd only have laughed.

Went for a walk this evening and soon fell in step with a rather bedraggled young woman whom I hadn't seen around the Tralee before. I noticed she had very dirty fingernails, which is one of my pet hates, but I tried not to hold that against her. We talked of one thing and another. Suddenly, out of the blue she said, 'Want to see my radiation burns?'

'Radiation burns?'

'This whole area is drenched with radiation. I don't know how or why, but I intend to find out, and you can help me.'

I assured her that I couldn't. I wished her well but declined the offer of seeing her burns, and made a hasty departure. I took her remarks with a pinch of salt. I thought she must have been drinking, or maybe she'd been reading the wrong newspapers. A lot of that sort of thing goes on these days.

I'm not saying she was wrong to worry about radiation, but I find that I can only worry about so many things at any one time. Of course I worry about the extinction of life on earth, but I also worry when the pilot goes out on the gas cooker. Sooner or later you have to be selective. And right now I've got quite enough worries to keep me going, without fretting about someone else's radiation burns.

As I hurried away the girl called after me, 'If that's your attitude then I hope you die of cancer.'

I don't think of myself as an old man, and yet I'm well aware that I'm probably over half-way through this thing we call life. I realise that there are certain options that are no longer available to me. There are some things I now know I'll never do or be.

I've decided to list a few.

And if you say that I could still do some of these things (go to the opera, for instance), all I can say is I know I won't because if you haven't been to the opera by the age of forty-five the chances are you never will.

Here goes.

> I will never go to the opera.
> I will never drive a Ferrari.
> No small child will ever again call me Daddy.
> I will never stand for Parliament or get into the Guinness Book of Records,
> I will never take recreational drugs.
> I will not become a teen-idol, a whizz-kid, an angry young man, a boy-genius, an *enfant terrible* or a soccer hooligan.
> I will never be considered precocious.
> Nobody will ever say I have an old head on young shoulders.
> I will never play for England at anything.
> I will not become accustomed to public speaking.
> I will never own a speedboat, an electric guitar or a set of dumb-bells.
> I will never have a face-lift.
> I will never visit a sauna.
> I will never go to Libya, Tonga, Tasmania or St Albans.
> I will never see the Hanging Gardens of Babylon, but I suppose there's some comfort in knowing that nobody else will either.
> I will not learn to play the oboe, take up tight-rope walking or participate in a new dance craze.
> I will not become an anthropologist, a martyr, an extrovert, a wit, or a pervert.
> I will not grow prize petunias.
> I will not go to a bullfight, a Hollywood première, a Shirley Bassey concert or an orgy.
> I will not develop a taste for advocaat.
> I will not, at this late stage, learn to love Ginger Rogers.
> And I'm never going to experience teenage angst,

and I'm never going to grow my hair over my ears or dye it strange colours, and I'll never wear two-tone shoes, and I'll never be initiated by an older woman.

> Above all, I will not leave a beautiful corpse.
> And you know what?
> I'm glad.

It's after midnight now. I'm dog-tired. I'd love to get some sleep but I just can't. Sometimes in all of this I can't help wondering if there isn't some kind of conspiracy going on against me. A conspiracy theory might explain everything, and I must say I wouldn't be at all averse to having everything explained.

Wouldn't it be nice if all my various tormentors gathered together and simply told me why they keep doing all these terrible things to me? I'd really like to know what I've done to deserve this.

But the worst thing of all is that when it comes right down to it I know that there *isn't* a conspiracy. There's no *reason* why these things keep happening to me. I've done *nothing* to deserve this.

I suppose everybody thinks they're unlucky. I suppose everybody thinks these things only happen to them. They think fate's singled them out for an extra dose of misfortune, but I don't think it has. There's nothing personal about fate. It's just a lottery. A certain number of people get cancer, a certain number go mad, a certain number lose their children in road accidents. And there's always a chance that you may be the unlucky person who gets cancer, goes mad and loses his children all on the same day; but that's all it is – chance.

I suppose there's a chance that tonight I might get a perfect night's sleep and wake up refreshed to enjoy the happiest day of my life. But somehow I doubt it.

Wednesday

I was woken very early this morning, not that I felt as though I'd ever been asleep, by all sorts of strange noises outside the caravan. There was hammering, the sound of a diesel engine, and electronic feedback. I thought it might be the Garcias trying to goad me, but I don't goad that easily. I turned over and tried to sleep, and who knows, I might have succeeded if the caravan door hadn't been flung open and Chief Inspector Hollerenshaw hadn't charged in brandishing a Japanese ceremonial sword.

'Now what?' I asked. I was really getting a bit irritated by Hollerenshaw.

'I'll give you "now what". I want some answers and I want them fast.'

'Go on then. Get it over with.'

'Good. Now first, if you want to persuade someone to do something, do you always tell them your real reasons for wanting it, or do you offer reasons which, although false, might prove more acceptable to that person?'

'I, well . . .'

'I'll give you "I, well"!'

He pressed the sword against my throat.

'Well no, not always I suppose.'

'Ha! Just as I thought. Now answer "true" or "false" to the following assertions; "Love is more important than success", "An accountant is more socially useful than a pop singer", "People who play practical jokes are compensating for weak personalities".'

It was all happening too fast for me to think about the answers, or in fact to think at all, but that didn't seem to worry Hollerenshaw, nor to slow him down.

'I'm now going to make certain statements. You have to

say whether you agree strongly, agree on the whole, neither agree nor disagree, disagree on the whole, disagree strongly. Ready?'

'Ready,' I said, though I wasn't.

'"National minorities have a right to self-government". "Greed is the main motivation for people who work hard". "Unemployment and social unrest are inevitable consequences of capitalism in decline".'

'You're out of your mind, Hollerenshaw.'

'I know that,' he said. 'I'm not stupid. Wait here.'

He dashed outside. I looked out to see what he was doing. I saw now that he'd arrived in a pick-up truck that had a number of huge stereo amplifiers and speakers mounted on the back. I saw him adjust the equipment, then pick up a microphone through which he spoke. His voice thundered through the speakers at painful volume.

'And now,' he said, 'for all our friends at the Tralee Carapark and Holiday Centre, one or two musical selections from *Don Giovanni*.'

I've never been a big opera fan, and *Don Giovanni* played at six in the morning, loud enough to distort the walls of your caravan is not my idea of the way to start the day. Hollerenshaw came into the caravan again.

'What price the Garcias now?' he said, chuckling insanely. 'Give me your wallet.'

I gave him my wallet. There was no point in arguing. He pulled a few notes from it and ate them.

Kathleen was wide awake by now. 'What's going on?' she asked.

I'd have liked to give her a simple answer.

'I'm helping the police with their enquiries,' I said.

Kathleen saw Hollerenshaw with a mouth full of chewed money, saw the ceremonial sword in his hand, and right away sensed something was wrong. She gave me a look as if to say, 'Don't worry. I can handle this,' and she said aloud, 'I think *I* can help the police far more with their enquiries than you can.'

She turned back the sheet to reveal that she was naked. She

shook her bare breasts in Hollerenshaw's direction. Kathleen is in many ways a remarkable woman, and I have to admire her for the supreme sacrifice she made by offering her body to Hollerenshaw. It was probably an old trick as far as the police are concerned, but it was a new one on me, and it certainly worked. Hollerenshaw became much calmer, even going so far as to throw aside the sword. Then he pulled down his trousers and mounted my trim and attractive wife.

Outside the caravan *Don Giovanni* grew louder. Hollerenshaw rutted fiercely in time with the music, and as he did so tears poured from his eyes, down his nose, and onto Kathleen.

'Oh Wolfgang, Wolfgang,' he murmured. 'Oh Albion!'

I thought Kathleen might have found this sort of verbal commentary a little surprising but she managed to take it in her stride. She was letting out some fairly choice epithets of her own.

I suppose many husbands in my position would have thought themselves perfectly justified in picking up the ceremonial sword and running Hollerenshaw through with it. But I'm not that sort of chap. Not yet, anyway. However, I will admit that I felt pretty uncomfortable standing in my own caravan like a spare part at the wedding. I left them to it.

As I stepped outside I heard, even above the sound of the opera, a familiar howling. In fact there were two distinct and separate howls. One belonged to Max, the other to Sinbad. My boy and his dog had been reunited in the wild. They came into view, Sinbad bounding over the earth, Max leaping from the roof of one caravan to the next. Many people would have looked at Max and seen an uncontrolled, deranged savage, but to me he was a sight for sore eyes.

'Max!' I said. 'I knew you'd be back.'

He jumped from the roof of our caravan into the cab of Hollerenshaw's pick-up truck. Sinbad jumped into the back and snarled at one of the speakers like an updated 'His Master's Voice' trademark. Max fired up the engine and set the truck in motion. The sound of Mozart diminished as he drove away, but I could still hear it far longer and louder than I really wanted to.

Soon, Hollerenshaw emerged from the caravan. He was

looking dishevelled and a little tear-stained, but nevertheless he was now placid and had the look of a man who'd pulled himself together.

'Just a couple more questions,' he said. 'Have you ever been troubled by necrophiliac fantasies?'

'Oh, leave me alone,' I said.

He kneed me in the groin as he had previously. I crumpled in pain.

'Second thing, make sure all your doors and windows are securely fastened before you turn in for the night. It's all right, I know that isn't a question.'

I didn't answer. I couldn't.

'I'll be off then. Mind how you go.'

I nodded in a way that suggested I would.

More news from home. Another phone message at the site office asking me to ring neighbour Ken, urgently.

'Don't tell me there's been another burglary, Ken? If so, I'll be home at once.'

At that moment returning home seemed like the best idea. Probably I should have done it days ago.

'No, I wouldn't do that, Eric. You see I phoned a few of these professional carpet-cleaning people and they were asking for silly money, so I thought sod that for a game of soldiers, I'll do the job myself, because I'm fairly handy at DIY, as you well know. Well, to cut a long story short, I had a bit of an accident with the cleaning chemicals.'

'Ah well,' I said, 'it can't be helped. They were rough old carpets anyway.'

'It was a fire Eric. It went up like matchwood.'

'What did? The carpet?'

'The house, Eric. It's gutted. It was a proper inferno. I was very lucky to get out alive. So you see, there wouldn't be much point in you rushing home, would there? And you know the funny thing is, my house wasn't damaged at all, even though we share a party wall.'

'There's a blessing,' I said.

'Obviously it's a bit of a setback but I'm here on the spot

and I've got everything in hand. If you give me the details of your insurance I'll start sorting it all out for you. Are you there, Eric?'

I was there but I wasn't saying anything. If Kathleen hadn't paid the insurance on the car, what was the likelihood of her having paid it on the house? I didn't want to think about it. I'd only worry, and I saw no point in letting a little thing like a gutted house spoil my holiday.

More aerial fun and games, and this time the air circus folk brought us memories of Vietnam. There were USAF helicopters, F-111s, B52s, napalm and defoliants. At least I assume they were using defoliants, either that or autumn has arrived very early this year.

I must say I've begun to think these chaps may be taking authenticity a little too far. I would write a strongly worded letter if I were the letter-writing type, and I'd definitely complain to my MP if I knew who he was.

History and education is all very well, but who knows where it will all end. Nerve gas? Chemical warfare? The massacring of villages? Radiation burns?

Then I remembered that I'd decided not to worry about radiation burns. It was a great weight off my mind. I reclined on the sun-lounger and mercifully, and a little surprisingly, I fell asleep.

It didn't last long. I woke with a start to find Max standing beside me.

'Max,' I said. 'It's good to see you again. Thanks a lot for what you did this morning.'

But Max wasn't very chatty. His face was set in an unattractive expression and I couldn't help noticing that he was holding a sharpened stake. It was about five feet long with dried blood on its point. Ceremonial swords, sharpened stakes; it was obviously going to be one of those days.

'What can I do for you, Max?'

He didn't reply, merely jabbed me with the stake and motioned for me to get up and start walking. I still had sleep in my eyes and my feet were bare, but Max made few concessions. He pushed me ahead of him at a cracking pace that had me stumbling frequently.

'What's all this about Max?' But answer came there none.

We came to a wood where Max let me stop walking. The trees were bare of course but the floor of the wood was thick with leaf-mould and old twigs. Max started scrabbling on the ground, clearing the debris to reveal a deep, narrow hole. It was only three feet across but must have been eight or nine feet deep. Max shoved me down the hole. It was cold and damp down there. The walls were smooth and there was no way of climbing out, and even if I'd been able to climb out Max was at the top ready to knock me down again.

'Max, old son,' I called, 'let's talk about this.'

In a sense we did. Max's head appeared over the rim of the hole and he said, 'I'm your nemesis, Dad. The earth demands a sacrifice.'

'Is something bothering you, Max? You can tell your old Dad about it. Together we'll thrash out a solution.'

Max didn't reply. His head disappeared. I couldn't even be sure if he was still there. The hole was far too deep to see out. Nothing happened for a while. Then I heard barking, then a dog's snout appeared over the edge of the hole. Saliva dripped down onto my face and Sinbad looked down on me, unsympathetically.

'Good dog,' I said.

Max reappeared and threw things down the hole at me, all kinds of things, few of them very agreeable. There was fresh blood, animal offal, bones and roots, the innards of a television set, some flat cider, scraps of wool and fur, even the odd herb and flower. He started to sing. That boy's never been a great one with a melody and his singing was tuneless and unpleasant, but I must admit he gave it his all. It had plenty of volume and it certainly seemed to come from the heart.

'Let me out of the hole, Max. There's a good chap.'

Somewhat to my surprise he did. His singing stopped and he gave me his hand so I could scramble up and out, but when I got out I wasn't sure that I was any better off than I had been down the hole. Max had been busy setting up a small altar bedecked with leaves and animal skulls. In the middle of it was a very passable wooden effigy of me.

'I have to kill you, Dad,' Max said calmly

'Come off it, Max. The joke's gone far enough.'

He beat me over the head. He knocked me almost senseless. He tied me to the altar, replacing the effigy with the real thing. He lit small fires round the altar and tossed the effigy into one of them. He produced a photograph of Joan Crawford, no doubt ripped from my coffee-table volume, and tore it into tiny pieces which he sprinkled over my head like confetti. Then he rubbed some kind of animal fat over my torso, and doused me with unusually strong-smelling urine. He then made a great show of sharpening a small but lethal-looking blade.

'We live in an age without ritual!' he shouted. 'We must make our own.'

'I'll buy you a sports car,' I pleaded. 'Only please let me go.'

'It is too late. The die is cast. The king must die!'

The king? Me?

Max raised his knife, and chanted. Things looked fairly bleak. The holiday looked as though it might be coming to a very abrupt end, and while I quite welcomed that, I didn't want my life to come to an abrupt end with it.

I know you're supposed to have some pretty profound feelings when you're facing death, but I can't say that I did. It occurred to me that if I'd spared the rod a bit less and tried to instill some discipline into Max this whole thing might never have happened; but even as I thought that, I knew it was a bit late in the day to be revising my views on child-rearing. I really did think I'd had my chips. But I'd reckoned without Sinbad.

As Max lowered the blade towards my heart, the dog leapt into the air, appeared to float for a moment or two, then snapped his teeth into Max's forearm. The momentum of the leap knocked Max to the ground where he and Sinbad rolled over and over in what looked very much like a life and death struggle.

'I pulled a thorn out of your foot,' Max yelled indignantly. 'You're supposed to be my friend forever.'

If Max had ever asked me for fatherly advice I'd certainly have told him never to trust a dog, but, of course, Max never *had* asked. There was much snarling and biting from both sides as the fight developed; not that I could see all of it from my position on the altar, and it wasn't very clear who was winning.

Naturally I had a certain parental sympathy with Max. I didn't want to see my own flesh and blood mauled to death by a dog. On the other hand I knew that if Max did win he'd most probably continue with his sacrifice of me, so I was rooting for Sinbad as well.

In fact I suspect Sinbad must have been getting the upper hand, because the moment Max was able to break free he scrambled to his feet and ran, with Sinbad in hot pursuit. They raced out of the wood and out of sight, and I was left alone.

This, of course, left me in a sticky position; not as sticky as before, but sticky all the same, and who knows how long I'd have stayed there, tied to the altar, if the cheery old chap with the radical views hadn't happened along. He may not be much of a cricket umpire, he may be a coward, and he may only be a theoretician, but he took one look at my plight and immediately grasped the situation.

'Human sacrifice eh?' he said as he untied me. 'These bloody kids. What'll they get up to next? I'd cut their stomachs open, put a maddened tarantula inside, then sew them up again.'

Even though I was fairly vexed with my boy Max, I felt I couldn't let the old chap's demented ramblings go entirely unchallenged.

'I'm sure the lad who did this had his reasons,' I said, being careful not to mention that it was in fact my own son who'd done it. 'The world is a very strange and difficult place for young people today.'

'Maybe,' he said, which was about the most liberal thing I'd ever heard him say. 'Maybe we should blame the parents. They're the ones I'd really like to get my hands on.'

I got back from the wood, much in need of a bit of tranquillity, and instead found Kathleen making the beast with two (or in this case I suppose three) backs, with the two dwarves who work in the entertainment field.

My suspicions should have been raised even before I entered

the caravan, by the sight of two miniature unicycles lying by the front step, but I thought nothing of it at the time. Then, as I opened the door, I saw two small, blue, sequinned jumpsuits on the carpet, but of course I assumed there would be a simple explanation. Even when I clapped eyes on the three of them shameless and inextricably intertwined in my own bed I couldn't be 100 per cent sure what they were up to. It isn't a thing you see every day. They might almost have been performing acrobatics, were it not for the fact that they were completely naked and one of the dwarves was performing oral sex on Kathleen.

I didn't want to come the heavy husband, and I really wasn't feeling strong enough to cope with a major confrontation, yet I felt that something had to be said.

'Put some clothes on please,' I suggested.

'Can't it wait a minute?' Kathleen asked breathily. 'We've very nearly finished.'

I can't deny that woman anything.

Afterwards the dwarves didn't have a lot to say for themselves and rode off unsteadily on their unicycles. Even Kathleen was reticent. I wondered if her experience with Hollerenshaw had, so to speak, primed the pump. I wondered whether to blame myself.

'I just wanted to see if it's true what they say about dwarves,' she said.

'Is it?'

'Yes.'

'Well, a lesson learned there,' I said curtly.

'Don't be such a spoil-sport, Eric,' she replied. 'If you can't let yourself go on your holidays then what are holidays for?'

I had no answer to that.

To be fair, Kathleen tried to make it up to me by cooking her stilton and sea-urchin surprise. I for one, however, got more of a surprise than I bargained for. Lurking under the cheese sauce, amid the tender morsels of delicately flavoured urchin, I came across what can only be described as a human finger.

I was pretty cut up about it. All my worst fears about finding something vile in my food were realised, but this was even worse because it was at my own table, in a meal that my own trim and attractive wife had lovingly self-catered.

'Well, I didn't put it there,' she snapped.

'Then how did it get there?'

'I don't know, Eric. And frankly I'm not very concerned. If you don't like my cooking you're free to go to the burger bar.'

'You might at least have the courtesy to apologise.'

'Love means never having to say you're sorry.'

She picked up the plate of food and shoved it in my face. The holiday seemed to have reached a new low.

It's after midnight now, and let's face it, it hasn't been a good day. Attempted human sacrifice, having your house gutted, threats with a Japanese ceremonial sword, attacks from the air, casual cuckoldry, fingers in your food, these things don't really leave you feeling at one with it all. They tend more to leave you feeling utterly destroyed.

In a perfect world I'd be sitting here now, possibly with a small whisky in my hand, possibly wearing a smoking-jacket, feeling calm and civilised, pen poised, all ready to reflect on my day and jot down *bons mots* about life in general. Instead, I'm sitting here more or less wishing I was dead.

My health hasn't picked up yet either. I've been having spells of double vision, fever, shooting pains in my arms and legs. I've developed some irregular purple spots all over my body, I cough up blood once in a while, and there's a strange growth at the base of my skull. At least nobody could any longer accuse me of just being a hypochondriac.

Basically I've had it up to here. I've had it up to higher than that. I've tried to be philosophical. I've tried to see the other chap's point of view. I've tried to look on the bright side, and I've tried not to let things get me down. And I'm sick and bloody tired of it!

I don't want to be decent and rational anymore. I can't see any future in it. I can't see any return. I want to rail against the world. I want to shout, 'Stop it'. I want to demand 'Why me?'

I want to say, 'Hey look, I've had enough of all this business. This just isn't bloody FAIR!'

I know life isn't meant to be fair, and I know a lot of people in the world are worse off than me. Though frankly I can't see very *many* being worse off than me. But in any case, so what? I don't really care about anybody else. They're just a bunch of arseholes anyway. And even if they were worse off than me, that wouldn't be any consolation. All I care about is me. All I want is a bit of consideration, a tiny bit of affection, a little bit of luck. What I really need is a good cry.

Nobody loves me. Nobody cares. I'm all alone in a rotten, vicious world. I don't like it. I didn't ask for it to be this way. I don't deserve it. I don't know why it has to be this way. I'm fed up. I'm lonely. I'm scared. I'm here, and I don't want to be here, and I'm miserable, and I'm pissed off, and I want everybody to know all about it.

I suppose I should feel better for having got that off my chest but I can't say that I do.

The day does seem, however, to have brought one bright spot. They say there's no rest for the wicked, but the way I see it the wicked do nothing but rest. To put it another way, Kathleen is sound asleep and doesn't look as though she'll be bothering me tonight. Maybe she's tuckered out after her exertions with Hollerenshaw and the dwarves. Maybe my irregular purple spots have put her off. But whatever the reason I'm very grateful for this small mercy. Is it just possible that things could be looking up?

Thursday

I woke up this morning, and frankly I wish I hadn't. I felt like death warmed up. Everything that could have gone wrong *had* gone wrong, although, having said that, I was sure there were plenty of other things that could still go wrong.

I didn't know what the day had in store for me but I was fairly confident that I wasn't going to like it. I was tempted to stay in bed all day, but I knew that terrible things were just as likely to happen to me there as anywhere else, and if there were any new catastrophes on the way I thought it best not to take them lying down.

I slipped out of bed without waking Kathleen and set off on a constitutional. I soon fell in step with the old chap with the radical views, who for all his many failings, at least knew an attempted human sacrifice when he saw one. We talked but I suspect I wasn't very good company.

'How's life treating you?' he asked.

'Pah!' I said.

'Life's a touchy subject is it?'

'I'll say.'

We walked on for a while but the conversation didn't exactly flow.

'I'm off to play bowls,' he said, holding up a leather case containing his woods.

'I've never played bowls,' I said.

'You haven't lived.'

'How true.'

We walked along some more until we could see the bowling-green in the middle distance. There was quite a crowd of old chaps gathered round the green, and even at this middle distance I could see they were all pretty agitated.

'Is it a tournament?' I asked.

'Tournament be blowed. There's something up.'

I've seldom seen a man of that age move with such speed and purpose. I certainly couldn't keep up with him. He arrived at the green some time before I did, and the moment he got there he seemed to be thunder-struck. He involuntarily dropped his woods and sank to his knees. His mouth opened in a silent scream. I couldn't immediately see the cause of his distress but then I caught sight of the bowling-green's turf and I was left in no doubt.

Someone had been at the green in the night and, using a turf-cutter, I suppose, had very carefully, and with some skill, cut a word into the surface with which I'd rather not sully my journal.

I thought I was almost past the point where I could be shocked or disgusted by anything, but somehow this crude act of vandalism got to me as much as anything I've been through in these recent days. I turned to the old chap. Tears cascaded down his face. I thought I was almost past being able to feel sympathy or concern for others, but the old lad's misery moved me no end.

I said, 'Why do people do things like this?'

He had a ready answer.

'Because people are scum, slime, faeces, mucus in the rectum of a tart who shags with donkeys.'

'You could be right,' I said.

'Of course I'm right.'

'But what's the answer?' I asked. 'Talking to them doesn't do any good. Reasoning doesn't do any good. I suppose you'd favour the electrodes in the genitals.'

'No. In this case I'd get a pair of metal funnels. I'd shove one in their mouths and the other up their backsides; and I'd pour red-hot chip fat down both funnels at the same time.'

Once I might have been horrified at such a suggestion. I'd have made all sorts of wishy-washy remarks about rehabilitation and re-education and violence begetting violence. Now it seemed like quite a good idea.

'Would you do that? Would you really?' I said.

'I most certainly would.'

'But only theoretically.'

'Yes,' he admitted.

'It's a good job there are some people in this world who are more than just theoreticians isn't it? People like Henry VIII, Pol Pot, Bob Geldof. People like me.'

I didn't know what I really meant by that at the time, but something was stirring inside me, something strange that I couldn't put a name to, but definitely something. I looked again at the old chap's face. I looked again at the wrecked bowling-green. I went back to my own caravan.

Kathleen had cooked something weird with eggs but I didn't touch it. I'd lost all sense of purpose, all direction, all sense of reality. And I'd certainly lost my appetite since finding the human finger.

I needed something to do, and sometimes there's nothing like a bit of housework to chase away the blues, so I attacked the caravan with mop, duster and vacuum cleaner. After a while the caravan looked lots better but I felt as bad as ever. Kathleen had watched me as she reclined on a bunk. She was swigging from a can of lager and she wasn't wearing much.

'Oh for God's sake Eric,' she said, 'give it a break. You're on holiday. Get out and enjoy yourself for once in your life.'

'Probably you just want to get rid of me so you can have your dwarves round.'

'If I wanted to have my dwarves round I wouldn't need any excuses. I just think you ought to get out for a bit. I'm only trying to show concern.'

Hell, it only went to show how much my perspectives had been distorted. I even mistrusted my own wife's compassion.

'You're like an overwound spring,' she said.

'Yes, that's just what I'm like. You're right. I need a break.'

I needed a holiday from my holiday. I hopped behind the wheel of the Wartburg. In the night someone had stolen the bonnet and headlights, and painted the words, 'Joan Crawford is sucking cocks in hell' along the side in black aerosol, but I didn't let that worry me.

I decided to go for a gentle cruise. I had a leisurely drive along the coast, just tooling along, minding my own business, keeping well within the speed limit. I can't say it cheered me up much. After a while I stopped, parked, got out, and breaking the habit of a lifetime, had a cheeseburger and a fizzy orange drink. It wasn't exactly wholesome but it seemed appropriate.

I understand they've done experiments with rats where they feed one lot on so-called junk food and another lot on food that's supposedly 'wholesome'. And it turns out that the lot fed on junk food live longer and have happier and healthier lives. Not that I know how you measure a rat's happiness. Not that I know how you measure anyone's happiness.

Sometimes I wonder if we humans aren't like rats in somebody's experiments. There's some mad scientist up in the sky who thinks to himself, 'Let's try another experiment on them and see what it does. Let's see how they behave if they have to live with nuclear war. Let's see how they handle another famine, a new disease, another earthquake, another hurricane, another flood.'

Well, in my opinion he ought to have got enough data by now not to need to do any more experiments like that. We all know what it does. It makes us bloody miserable, that's what it does. Sending down wars or plagues or acts of God just kills a lot of people and makes the rest of us feel even more pissed off and desperate than we did before. He ought to know that by now. Maybe this is sacrilege. Maybe this is bad-mouthing God. Just as well that Sally isn't around to hear me saying any of it.

So I walked along the beach. There were a few kids playing, some blokes riding horses, a couple having a picnic, but I didn't take a lot of notice. I was deep in thought. My hands were in my pockets and I was kicking an old 'Fairy' bottle across the sand.

It was then that I had what can only be described as an apocalyptic vision. It sounds silly I know, but that's exactly what it was. Some people would probably call it a moment in and out of time, and I wouldn't argue with that. Anyone who's ever had an apocalyptic vision will tell you that it's a pretty tricky experience to put into words, but here goes.

I kicked the Fairy bottle into the sea and looked out to the horizon. Suddenly the sea turned violent purple, much like the shade that Kathleen's been painting her nails lately, and started to heave into mountainous waves. In no time at all it was actually boiling. Something told me this was more than just a bit of freak weather. The clouds flew across the sky at a rate of knots and turned jet-black so that they blotted out the sun. A wind got up. It was icy cold. It whipped at my clothes and went at my cheeks like sandpaper.

Hideous incorporeal demons rose out of the sea, darting back and forth all over the heavens, raging, screaming, making an unearthly din that forced me to put my hands over my ears. There was a flash of light, a flash like you've never seen, a lightning bolt big enough to smash the world you'd think, and a peal of thunder that shook the ground and hurt my eardrums even though they were covered.

After that noise there was suddenly a great calm and quietness. The sea went smooth as glass, and gradually out of that quietness I could hear a heavenly chorus. At first it was just a soft, wordless, gentle singing, but it grew louder and I quite distinctly heard my name being chanted by a heavenly host. 'Eric, Eric,' they sang.

I don't know what came over me next, but I waded into the sea and got very emotional. A galleon appeared on the horizon, cutting through the waves like a knife, glowing with unearthly light. Angels filled the air. Sea-monsters popped their heads through the surface of the water. The firmament trembled. Sheets of fire danced across the sky; and I know this will sound silly, but I fell on the sand and started speaking in tongues. I dare say I wailed and gnashed my teeth as well, but I don't remember more than that.

Afterwards I was a bit embarrassed by the whole thing. The couple who'd been having the picnic looked fairly embarrassed as well. It appeared that I was the only one who'd seen the apocalyptic vision. The couple hadn't noticed a thing, except me rolling around on the beach and making a display of myself.

The woman said, 'Are you all right?'

'I suppose so,' I said. 'I've just been transported. I've had a vision.'

'We've got a first-aid box in the car.'

'I'm not hurt. I feel fine. In a way I've never felt better in my life. This is what I came on holiday for. This is what I came on the planet for.'

'We're just here for the nightlife and the seafood.'

'Nightlife and seafood have their place in things too,' I said.

'You've never said a truer word.'

And she was right. I hadn't. My apocalyptic vision had obviously brought wisdom with it. I was pleased as punch.

Once the vision was over and I'd got my breath back there wasn't much else to do except get in the car and go back to the Tralee. I felt I ought to tell someone about what I'd just been through, but I wasn't sure whom. There was no talking to my near and dear ones these days even if I could find them. Maybe I was better keeping it under my hat.

I was still a bit shaken so I was driving slowly and trying to keep out of harm's way. I kept well over so that people could overtake me without difficulty. However, when I got to a stretch of road where overtaking wasn't so easy, some boy-racer type got right behind me and started flashing his lights and sounding his horn. I was dashed if I was going to be forced into driving faster than I wanted to in my delicate state so for a mile or two we carried on in this manner. I drove slowly and with infinite care while this maniac behind me flashed and hooted and generally made a road-hog of himself.

Eventually I'd had enough so I pulled over on the grass verge, stopped my car and waved him on. There was a great grinding of gears and squealing of tyres and he ploughed right into the back of the Wartburg. I had a feeling of *déjà vu*.

I know only too well how little bangs and scrapes to their cars can get people excited, so I wasn't too surprised when the boy-racer got out of his car and came over to abuse me.

'You tosser. You wanker. You old fart. You senile git.' That sort of thing.

When you're fresh from an apocalyptic vision you can take this sort of thing in your stride. It was all water off a duck's back to me. I waited very calmly and had a good look at my abuser. He was young of course, not more than twenty, and that seems very young indeed when you're forty-five and feel yourself to be possessed of a superior wisdom. He was dressed trendily and had styled hair and sunglasses and white shoes. He was also rather small and feeble-looking and he had a thin, whiny voice. He was starting to irritate me.

'Please shut up,' I said.

'Don't tell me to shut up, you ponce,' he said.

Then he clenched his fists and waved them in my face, which as it turned out was a bit silly of him. I don't know whether my vision had given me hidden strength, or made me intolerant of fools, or what, but I looked at him and I thought, 'You don't have to put up with this, Eric.' I took my time, waited for an opportunity, drew back my fist, and hit him on the nose. It looked as though it hurt. He grabbed his nose with both hands, so I punched him in the belly.

'All right, all right,' he said. 'Stop it. I'm sorry I ran into your car, really. Just don't hit me any more. I'm sorry.'

I'm not the vindictive sort and I could see that the lad was suffering a bit so I helped him into his car. That was when his troubles really started. I glanced into the car and saw a few lumps of turf on the back seat. There was also what I took to be a turf-cutter. I made him open the boot. That was also full of turf. I pulled out the turf and arranged it at the roadside so it spelled that word I'd rather not sully my journal with. I remembered the bowling-green. I remembered those old chaps who'd had their game of bowls ruined. I thought of the viciousness and the stupidity and the desecration. Then I hit the lad some more.

'Get in the passenger's seat,' I said. 'I'm driving.'

We drove off. The lad asked if I was taking him to the police.

'No such luck,' I said.

I found a pet shop not too far away. I took the lad's money from him and bought half a dozen rats.

'Do they bite?' I asked the assistant.

'Only if they're angry.'

'What gets them angry?'

'Being tormented, not being fed, being kept in a confined space. Why?'

I paid for my rats and returned to the car. I drove until I

found a deserted lay-by then hit the lad a bit more. I think he started to cry. I made him get into the boot of his car. He did as he was told. He'd have crawled on his hands and knees from Mablethorpe to Skegness if I'd told him to. Then I tormented the rats for a while and threw them into the boot after the lad. I slammed the boot shut and locked it. The rats might not be hungry now but they'd get peckish sooner or later.

I had quite a long walk back to my car but I didn't mind. On the way I wondered if I'd been a bit soft on the lad. Perhaps, in a perfect world, I should indeed have gone for the funnels and the red-hot fat, but we don't live in a perfect world. However, as I drove back to the Tralee Carapark and Holiday Centre it felt a little more perfect than it had before. I also wondered if I'd been a bit hard on the rats, but at least I no longer felt like an overwound spring.

I went for an early evening smoke in the toilet and shower block and found to my horror, though scarcely to my surprise, that vandals had been at their sorry work there too.

Mirrors had been smashed, paper towels strewn around, plugs had been stolen from the sinks and there were graffiti everywhere. The walls of my favourite cubicle now had crude drawings of male and female organs on them, done in such a way as to suggest a lack of familiarity with the real thing. There were messages along the lines of, 'My name's Brian. I like a bit of strap. Make date', slogans about football teams, racial slurs and various invitations to all sorts of unlikely and illegal sexual jamborees.

I entered a cubicle, sat down and lit up, but the magic had, to a very large extent, gone. Then I noticed that someone had made a hole in the side wall of the cubicle and under it had written, 'Glory Hole. Suck here.' I didn't immediately catch the significance of that, but it wasn't long before the significance was rammed home in no uncertain fashion. I was about two-thirds of the way through my cigarette when a penis, erect, hefty and unmistakably homosexual, popped through the aforementioned hole and waved at me.

I'm a permissive sort of a chap and I don't really mind what people do by prior arrangement in the comfort of their own homes. However, the episode in which I seemed to have become enmeshed was not by prior arrangement and was certainly not in the comfort of anyone's home.

I began by thinking, 'Ignore it and it'll go away,' but I ignored it and it didn't go away. In fact, if anything, the offending article seemed to be making its presence ever more keenly felt. It was quite putting me off my smoke. Then a voice from the other side of the wall said, 'Go on Marjory, slip it in,' and that did it. Nobody calls me Marjory and gets away with it, not anymore. My smoking pleasure had been thoroughly ruined so I stubbed out what remained of the cigarette, right where it hurts. It did me good to stop being a 'niceguy'.

When I got back to the caravan Kathleen had made me a haddock and cowheel ragout. Possibly I was still haunted by the human finger incident, possibly my appetite had been ruined by the cheeseburger and fizzy drink, but whatever the reason, I felt that the dish had failed to come up to Kathleen's normal high standards and I didn't see any point pretending otherwise. Now, more than ever, I didn't want us to have any secrets from each other.

'This is rubbish,' I said.

'If you don't want to eat it you know what you can do,' she replied spiritedly.

I knew exactly what I could do. There was something in her voice that got me riled. The red mist swam before my eyes and my brain seethed. I flung the plate of food across the caravan. I banged my fist on the table, whipped out my wedding tackle and said commandingly, 'Eat this, bitch!'

Even as I said it I wasn't sure what had come over me. I definitely wasn't myself, but actually I was rather glad not to be myself; and fortunately Kathleen was more than happy to oblige. We went on to have what can only be described as a damn good bout of mixed wrestling.

I'm not the sort of man who's given to idle boasting about his sexual prowess and expertise, but on this occasion I can say in all modesty that I excelled myself. In fact I think I must have excelled most of the chaps walking on the face of the earth.

I had a rod of iron, of finely tempered steel, and I employed it with a canny mixture of subtlety and ruthlessness. It all came to me instinctively. I knew all the positions, all the moves, all the zones. Let's face it, I was a sex machine. Certainly after three hours or so I had Kathleen saying she couldn't take any more, and it's been a long time since I, or anyone else, has been able to do that. Afterwards she was a quiet and contented woman. She even had a bit of a look of Joan Crawford about her.

It's after midnight now. Kathleen is sound asleep. In the distance I can hear howling. I can't be sure whether it's Max or Sinbad. Somewhere out there Sally may well be lecturing a group of Hell's Angels on the error of their ways.

This is our thirteenth day at the Tralee. The holiday is nearly over. Mostly it's been a bit of a pain in the neck, a long series of disasters and humiliations. Yet as I sit here now, calmly writing these words, I feel on top of the world. In fact I've never felt better in my life. All the aches and pains, the cramps and spasms and irregular purple spots have gone. All the old worries and wild questionings have disappeared completely. How come?

Well partly it must have something to do with the romp of a lifetime that I've just had with Kathleen, partly it must be the apocalyptic vision, but mostly I think it's this: that which does not destroy us makes us strong.

I've been through quite an ordeal, almost like some strange initiation ceremony. It has shaken and terrified me, brought me near to madness and destruction, but I've survived, and I am now mighty and impregnable. Everyone and everything have done their worst to me, but I'm still here. What else can happen to me? What else is there to fear? I am undefeated. I am strong, wise and glorious. I feel like a bit of a superman. Something tells me that tomorrow could be quite a day. It's time to get some sleep. Even supermen need their eight hours.

Friday

Woke up this morning from a deep and dreamless sleep and decided they all had to die.

The day was perfect; calm, clear and golden. I still felt like a million dollars. I was happy, secure, a man at the height of his powers. All that spoiled things was the vile, stinking mass of humanity that crawled and grubbed upon the earth. Maybe it was bloodlust, maybe it was delusions of grandeur, a feeling of being beyond good and evil, but, whatever the reason, I knew that a certain species of vermin had to be purged from the face of the globe; and I was just the man to do the purging.

I stepped out of bed and looked at myself in the mirror. Now there were no doubts or uncertainties, no hesitations, no taste of ashes in the mouth. Now I liked what I saw. It was the body and form of a God, albeit a forty-five-year-old God. Kathleen pretty much confirmed this by asking me to take her again on the caravan floor several times, but I had to be stern.

'Please Kathleen,' I said, 'not now. I have a higher purpose.'

I did, however, let her run her hands adoringly over my flanks, and anoint me with costly oils and scented balms. I let her dress me in loose clothing. I let her strap a small, improvised armoury about my person; kitchen-knives, a hammer, an axe, a crow-bar, Max's old catapult, the ceremonial sword that Hollerenshaw had left behind, and a cricket bat. It was a little primitive but it would do the job. I let Kathleen kiss my feet before putting on a pair of stout walking-boots. I couldn't deny that I still felt a certain affection for the woman.

'Perhaps I shall spare you after all,' I said to her.

'Thank you, Master.'

Kathleen certainly knew how to talk to a husband now. I

gave her a goodbye peck. I stepped from the caravan dressed for action, a war machine, a fighting man from head to toe.

I started small. I set out to find Kathleen's dwarves. They were outside their caravan practising headstands and comical falls. I must say they looked very smart in their jumpsuits, their sequins glittering in the early morning sun.

'So it's true what they say about dwarves, is it?' I said. I didn't have time for pleasantries.

'That depends what you've heard,' one of them said. They both giggled.

'I've heard the lot.'

'You must be a very good listener.'

'Not really. For instance, I've heard more than I want to hear from you two.'

They both laughed this time. I didn't know what was so funny. I wasn't very interested in finding out.

'I'll teach you to make the beast with two backs with my trim and attractive wife,' I said.

'We don't need any teaching.'

They got fairly hysterical about that. They thought it was the best joke yet; but I'd had enough. If there's one thing I can't stand it's a pair of acrobatic dwarves from the entertainment field who've performed adultery with my wife and who have puerile senses of humour.

I invited them to step inside their caravan. They didn't much want to go, but I picked them up and threw them in. They landed lightly on their feet, athletic to the end. I carved them up with a kitchen-knife. They were filleted, gutted and chopped into bite-size pieces. They died with a certain grace and acrobatic skill, but they had performed their last tumbles.

It was still early when I arrived at the site shop. The door was locked but the youth was visible behind the counter, reading his morning paper. He still looked pretty sullen despite his recent wage increase. I tapped on the glass but he wouldn't open up. He gave me an insolent stare and pointed to his watch to indicate that he wouldn't be opening the shop for another fifteen minutes. I wasn't having any of that. I swung my axe and smashed down the shop door. Glass and wood splinters exploded into the shop. The youth looked up. He seemed impressed. His facial expression almost changed.

'Hey, all right,' he said, looking at the axe with some admiration. 'That's some fine political weapon you've got there. You could implement a lot of new policies with that.'

'I intend to.'

'Like what?'

'The first thing I intend to do is get a bit of decent service in this shop.'

He almost smiled. For a second he must have thought I was joking. Then I heaved the axe round in a big circle and destroyed a shelf of tinned plum tomatoes just inches from the youth's head. Then he knew I wasn't joking.

'I want a bit of please and thank you,' I said. 'I want a bit of, "Can I help you sir?" and, "Much obliged sir, will there be anything else?" and, "Nothing's too much trouble sir," and, "It's a pleasure to be of service sir." And I want a bit of bowing and scraping and touching the forelock and a bit of "the customer's always right".'

I chopped the counter into smithereens and he seemed to understand me. For the next ten minutes or so we played a little charade, and I must admit the sullen youth wasn't bad at all. He enquired after my health, commented on the weather, and hoped I was having a pleasant holiday. He assured me that oranges were cheap and plentiful, and that corned beef was down in price for just one week. He carefully wrapped my selection of goods. He gave me a free carrier bag and offered to deliver to my caravan. He was everything that anyone's ever wanted in a shop assistant. Of course he was a little nervous, and he'd broken out in a cold sweat, but that was only to be expected.

I told him it wouldn't be necessary for him to deliver to my caravan. I told him he wasn't going anywhere.

'You know your problem?' I asked.

'No.'

'No *sir*,' I corrected.

'No sir.'

'The problem is that you seem to think politics is a complete answer. I'm here to tell you that it isn't.'

'Then what is, sir?'

'*I* am the complete answer.'

Then I hacked him to death. It sounds easy when you put it like that. It wasn't. It was fairly hard work actually, and it was just as well that I was fit, strong and in prime condition. The sullen youth tried to run of course, which didn't make the job any easier. As he ran he knocked down displays of curried beans and spaghetti hoops. I finally cornered him by the frozen foods, and finished him off by the soap powders and toilet rolls. His final words were, 'Will there be anything else, sir?'

When I came to my friend, the personable stutterer, he was still struggling to repair his strafed lilo. I told him life was too short to mess about trying to repair strafed lilos.

'You could b-b-be right. Easier to b-buy a new one in the long run.'

'There is no long run,' I said, but for obvious reasons he didn't catch my drift.

'I've b-been thinking about my f-f-f-future.'

'Oh yes?'

'B-B-Bingo calling, v-v-v-voice-overs, they're not f-f-f-f-for me.'

'They're certainly not.'

'Reckon I'll b-b-become a sign-writer.'

'A bit late,' I said.

'B-B-Better late than never.'

'I don't know,' I said. Then I said something that took him by surprise. 'Show me your tool.'

'What?'

I repeated my request. He was reluctant, shy. He probably suspected my motives. Then I told him to whip it out and whip it out quick or I'd pull his face off with my hammer. He unzipped himself and unfurled his penis. It was much as I'd expected. It was definitely well above average in size, and it had a cigarette burn on it.

'You're a damn fool,' I said. 'With a little common sense and a little self-knowledge you could have been a very happy man. Instead you became neurotic. You worried about all the wrong things. You had all sorts of stupid ambitions for jobs that you couldn't possibly do. You've got a penis many a chap would be envious of, yet you worry about the length of it, not that length's important anyway, and you stick it through holes in toilet walls. Well, it's asking for trouble isn't it? You're an idiot. You don't deserve to live. I'm going to put you out of your misery.'

'Be reasonable,' he pleaded. 'Be fair. Don't be a bastard.'

'Say that again.'

He was only too happy to. He probably thought I was weakening. He probably thought I was showing sympathy. I wasn't. I was just fascinated to see how his stutter disappeared when he had something real to worry about. It wasn't much consolation for him of course. I ran him through with the ceremonial sword, and he never really enjoyed the benefits of normal speech. Still, at least he'd enjoyed them for about thirty-five seconds, and, as he might well have said himself, better late than never.

The cheery old chap with the radical views was next on my list. I knocked politely on his caravan door, and he let me in. He was having a late breakfast. He offered me a piece of his bacon sandwich, and in order to lull him into a false sense of security, I accepted. In the old days I wouldn't have touched it, but I was feeling reckless, also I suppose once you've found a human finger in your food, the odd human hair doesn't hold so many horrors. We talked about the rights of the unborn child, pensions, the mass media, and bowls.

'I don't think you'll have any more trouble in the bowls department,' I said.

I explained that I'd caught the young villain who'd vandalised the bowling-green, and taught him a bit of a lesson.

'Did you give him the old funnels and red-hot chip fat treatment?'

I explained that I'd had to improvise with whatever materials came to hand.

'Improvisation's too good for them,' he said. 'Pity you didn't have this.'

He scrabbled around in a kitchen cabinet and brought out an M-16 rifle. He patted it lovingly, held it up to the light, showed me how to assemble and load it. Then he handed it to me so I could feel its balance and elegance of design.

'Lovely bit of weaponry,' he said.

'Lovely if you've got the guts to use it. But you haven't, have you?'

'I might have if it came to it.'

'No. You're just a helpless, frightened, essentially fascist, hollow man.'

'Aren't we all?'

'No,' I said.

I fired the M-16. A volley of bullets stitched the old man to the wall of his caravan. He'd seen the limitations of theory. He'd made his last bad umpiring decision.

I was tempted to take the M-16 and polish off the rest of the inhabitants of the Tralee Carapark and Holiday Centre without so much as breaking into a sweat; but they could wait. I had other plans, wider horizons.

I tossed the weapon in the back of the Wartburg and hit the road. I drove fast and mercilessly until I came to the Pump Inn. It had just opened. There was a car parked in front which looked ominously familiar. It had been resprayed, given alloys and a go-faster stripe, but I knew what was mine.

I peered into the pub and saw him; so-called Honest Iago. He was in high spirits. He was leaning on the bar. He had a floozy with him, and he was drinking something fancy from a funny-shaped glass. He looked ready to die. I returned to the car that had once been mine. I slipped under it and made a few modifications to the braking system. I lurked in the pub car-park, waiting and watching for Honest Iago and his floozy to emerge. I didn't have to wait long. They came out of the Pump Inn, all Latin affection and cheap laughter, though perhaps you can't put a price on laughter. They looked as happy as people like that ever do, but I knew it wasn't real happiness because real happiness lasts, and theirs wasn't going to.

He started his car, my car. He drove a little too flashily and a little too fast. He left the car-park and drove out of sight. I listened. Seconds later I heard the terrible cawing of tyres, a heavy metallic thud, a chorus of shattering glass, as the car failed to negotiate a corner and made lethal contact with another vehicle.

I went to look at the accident. I was one of a crowd. Honest Iago had collided with a nippy little sports car that contained two women in Girl Guide uniforms. He hadn't been wearing a seat-belt and had been thrown through the windscreen. He was dead all right. His slick hair was bejewelled with fragments of glass. The women in the nippy little sports car were alive but badly injured, and imprisoned in the wreckage. There was liquid everywhere; blood on the dashboard and steering-wheel, engine coolant from the radiators, petrol on the road. I lit a cigarette, tossed the match aside casually, and beat a hasty retreat. Both cars exploded in flame. The other spectators hit the pavement. A cloud of greasy black smoke rolled into the sky. I had to laugh.

I got in the Wartburg and drove to the Police Station. I parked opposite and waited for Hollerenshaw to finish his shift. As he left the building I saw him say the kind of goodbyes to people that suggested he'd finished for the day. Little did he know.

I expected him to drive home, but in fact he walked, so I followed on foot. We soon arrived at his house, easy walking distance from work, very convenient. It was a solid end-of-terrace house, grey, ordinary, unostentatious, the house of an honest copper. He walked briskly up the short garden path. His key turned in the lock. He didn't notice that I'd crept up behind him, silently and stealthily. He opened the door and he was still unaware of my presence, but then he felt the harsh pressure of the rifle at the base of his spine, and he must have felt my breath on the back of his neck, and certainly he heard me say, 'One word out of you, Hollerenshaw, and you'll never hear another note of Mozart.'

We went in. The living-room was spacious, though the

furnishing was impractical and difficult to keep clean, I'd have thought. The carpet was cream. The bookcases and tables and sideboard were white lacquer. There were pictures of sailing ships on the walls, a white upright piano with framed snapshots of cats on top of it.

'You live alone?' I asked.

'Yes. Nobody'll have me.'

'Can't say I'm altogether surprised.'

Along one wall of the room was a big stereo and a vast collection of records, mostly classical, mostly Mozart.

'Why don't you put on a little background music?' I said. 'Some Wolfgang if you like.'

'Mozart can never be mere background music,' he said, but all the same he put on a record. I think it was *The Magic Flute*. I turned the volume up loud. I told Hollerenshaw not to make any sudden moves.

'I realise that the police have a difficult job to do,' I said. 'I know there's a lot of danger and a lot of pressure. I know it's hard on the nerves, on marriages, on personal relationships in general.'

He nodded.

'But that still doesn't explain why you're the sort of maniac who eats people's money, threatens them with a ceremonial sword, and then has it off with their wives.'

He hung his head. I asked him about his early years, his relationship with his mother and father, his first sexual experiences, his school career. We discussed his social and political attitudes, his sense of humour, his dealings with colleagues, his emotional stability. I interpreted some of his dreams for him. I'd have liked to show him some ink blots and see what he made of them, but that wasn't really necessary. I'd already come to the conclusion that Hollerenshaw was just a raving nutter. In other circumstances I might have been more sympathetic. I usually have a lot of time for the mentally ill. But not today.

The music played, and before long he was blubbing. But he blubbed a lot more when I started to take his Mozart records out of their inner sleeves and inflicted deep grooves and scratches on them with the nose of the M-16, before tossing them into the fireplace.

'Please,' he said, 'I know I'm not a good man. I know I'm guilty, as guilty as any of the villains I've put away, guiltier than some, but please, please, leave Mozart alone. You can have anything you want; money, drugs, girls, nicked microwaves, anything.'

I was unmoved. What would I want with a microwave? I continued ruining his records. The music swelled and drowned the noise of his pathetic whining and pleading. It also drowned the noise of rifle shots as they whipped through Hollerenshaw's body and lodged in the thick padding of his white settee.

'What about the new Albion?' he asked as he expired.

'I'll give you "Albion",' I said feelingly.

Fortunately the bullets hadn't damaged Hollerenshaw's police-badge. I had a use for that. I took it from his pocket and slipped it into my own. It came in very handy when I got to the local airfield. I waved the badge around, and although there was a certain amount of suspicion and resentment, doors certainly opened.

I told some uniformed official that I wanted to talk to the stunt flyers from the air circus, and I was led out to a hangar where half a dozen chaps in bomber-jackets, with mustaches, swept-back hair, and public school accents and manners, were tinkering with historic aircraft and sipping martinis.

'I'm in a bit of a spot, actually,' I said to them, trying to adopt their vernacular. 'The local force has made a bit of a bish of things, and I know you fellows will be only too happy to help the forces of law and order.'

'Hear, hear.'

'The simple fact is, I need a chopper, a canister of napalm and a chap with nerves of steel. I wonder if I've come to the right place.'

They were a rugged devil-may-care sort of bunch and I had no difficulty finding a volunteer. In fact they almost came to blows deciding who should have the pleasure of taking me up.

We combed the area at treetop height. The helicopter was a dodgy old thing, and in normal circumstances I'd never have dreamed of going up in it. We saw beaches, caravans, roads, some tennis-courts, a couple of bowling-greens, a traffic jam, a swimming-pool; and then I saw what I was looking for.

On a stretch of dirty beach there were a dozen or more motorcycles parked in a circle, and inside that circle there was a group of unsavoury, beleathered bikers. I peered at them through binoculars. They were the group who'd roughed me up at the Tralee. They were still drinking and smoking hand-rolled cigarettes. Some were revving their bikes, a couple were throwing a frisbee. There was no sign of my lovely daughter Sally.

The helicopter hovered above them. Sand was whipped around. They couldn't ignore it. They looked up, unsure if we were friendly or not. Somebody waved. Then I let them have it with the napalm. Fiery, liquid death fell from the sky. They ran but they couldn't hide. They tried to escape to the sea, but my pilot skimmed along the water's edge and drove them back up the beach.

I got the pilot to set me down some way from the mayhem. We shook hands. I gave him a filled hip-flask as a way of saying thank you. He took a manly swig before saluting and flying off. I walked towards the burnt bodies and flaming motorcycles. I remembered the cigarette burns on my chest. They felt like medals now. One of the bikers was still alive, just, crawling through the sand towards me. He looked at me with pained, empty eyes, and said, 'Which chapter are you with?'

'The final chapter,' I said.

In the distance a helicopter crashed. The drink in the hip-flask was poisoned. The chaps from the flying circus may have been a good bunch in their way, but as far as I was concerned they were just air pollution.

I took a walk along the beach to recharge my batteries. I must have sauntered for a mile or so, and I'd probably have walked miles further if I hadn't come across an all too familiar caravan. It was the pink, Georgian-windowed, shuttered, chromed, wood-panelled affair belonging to the Joan Crawford look-alike. How it came to be parked on a public beach I didn't know, but business had obviously been brisk. The sand was well churned up by footprints leading to and from the door.

More interesting, there was an almost equally familiar blue van parked beside it, which I was certain belonged to the man who'd conned me into buying a raffle ticket and becoming Sinbad's owner. The van was empty. Sinbad's raffler was inside the caravan, either getting the shock of his life, or getting exactly what he wanted.

I reckoned both of them deserved to become victims of my wrath, but I wasn't sure how to do it fittingly. I needn't have worried. Fate lent a hand. I heard manic barking behind me, and turned to see Sinbad bounding over the sand. He seemed utterly out of control. The legs were unco-ordinated and the eyes were unfocused, but he still didn't look like an easy touch. In fact he looked ready to tear the innards out of anything that stood in his path.

'Here boy,' I called.

He came readily enough. He leapt at me. I dodged his snapping jaws. I pulled open the door to the fancy caravan, bundled Sinbad inside, and slammed the door after him. There was some prolonged screaming from inside, and someone tried to wrestle the door open; but I held it secure.

'Kill boy!' I shouted to Sinbad.

And I've every reason to believe that Sinbad did what he was told.

I was late for the start of *Skegness Stars*. I managed to miss the singer of 'I am Sixteen Going on Seventeen', the xylophone player, and the comedian. That didn't break my heart. The second half was just starting so I sat in the bar until I heard the music that introduced the hypnotist.

He'd barely made his entrance and begun his patter before I burst into the auditorium. There was some surprise and a certain amount of tittering as I careered down the centre aisle and climbed onto the stage. I brandished my M-16. The audience seemed to think it was all part of the show. The hypnotist knew better.

'What do you think you're doing?' he said.

'I'm going to give a little demonstration of mind control,' I replied.

He was staring at me fixedly. I think he was trying to hypnotise me, but I was no longer the impressionable subject I'd been on my last stage appearance.

'Hypnotism is a fine art,' I said. 'It exercises power over the human mind. It makes the subject highly suggestible. The hypnotist is able to make the subject do all sorts of things he wouldn't normally do. It sounds impressive, but I can do much the same with this rifle.'

I pumped a few rounds into the stage. The hypnotist began to tap dance, and at my suggestion he went into a full-blown version of 'On the Good Ship Lollipop'. The audience lapped it up. Poor fools.

'Now you're a mountain climber and you're going to scale Everest.'

He shinned up the mouldings of the stage arch to the boxes at the side of the auditorium, into the balcony, then higher and higher still until he was up in the Gods.

'Now you think you're Superman,' I said. 'We're all going to see you fly.'

He didn't want to jump so I fired in his general direction. I don't think I hit him, but the shock was enough to make him lose his grip and come tumbling head first down into the middle stalls. Of course, unlike myself, he wasn't Superman. His wretched, broken body showed no signs of life.

By now the audience had realised that not everything they'd seen was strictly in the script. I tried to make my escape. I had to shoot down a few audience members who were on their feet and blocking the exit, and I had to take out the stage crew, the house manager, and a couple of usherettes before my path was clear. The punters were in some disarray, yelling and screaming, in some cases for their money back. I don't know what they were complaining about. They'd seen something genuinely unrepeatable.

Outside the night was soft. There was a full moon. I stole a car and returned to the Tralee.

They all had to go. They all had to fall victim to my irresistible will. Babies, children, teenagers, adults, senior citizens, all the inhabitants of the Tralee Carapark and Holiday Centre; I blew them all away like dust. They were dog food. They were nothing. They never had a chance. They never deserved one.

But there was one pair that I saved till last. You might have thought that with all the rifle shots and all the screams, and all the begging for mercy, even the Garcias might have noticed that something was going on. But they didn't. Their caravan door remained closed. Music continued to blast out from behind it. They never saw me coming.

I admit that I hadn't heard too much from them lately. There'd been some uncontrolled laughter and relentless, loud bursts of Herb Alpert, and a growing pile of liquor bottles tossed under their caravan; but by their standards, this was fairly civilised behaviour. I marched up to the caravan and broke a couple of windows. I didn't have time for formal invitations. From inside, above the music, I could hear muffled wailing. I didn't like the sound of that at all.

At last Garcia opened the door. He was wearing a butcher's apron and surgical gloves, and he was spattered with blood.

'Just what exactly's going on in there?' I demanded.

At least he had the decency to look lost for words. He shrugged his shoulders. He looked furtive.

'Nothing much, gringo. We're just preparing a barbecue.'

I wasn't satisfied with his answer. I picked up my cricket bat and played a firm hook shot to Garcia's head. It knocked him for six. I strode into the caravan. Mrs Garcia tried to block my way. She was naked but for a tutu, fishnets and a surgical mask. I pushed her aside, turned off the music, and surveyed the grim scene. There was medical equipment everywhere – syringes, scalpels, saws, tourniquets, drips, X-rays, machines for measuring heart-beat, brain waves, blood pressure, an autoclave. And in the midst of all this, set on a Formica kitchen-table, were three largish inverted goldfish bowls, each containing a severed human head. There was a tangle of wires and tubes that ran from the heads to beneath the table where they were connected to batteries, pumps, and what looked like a demijohn of home brew.

That would have been rum enough, but rummer still was the fact that each head seemed to be alive. The eyes blinked, the mouths moved, the skins appeared to be well supplied with blood. Rummest of all, I recognised one of the heads. It belonged to Terry, my former colleague, now my successor in the bought ledger office of a major chain of furniture retailers.

'You butchers! You maniacs!' I shouted at the Garcias.

Mr Garcia had recovered somewhat from the blow I'd given him, and he staggered towards me.

'I'm afraid you've seen too much,' he said.

I didn't know about that, but I'd certainly seen more than enough. As he lunged at me I picked up a scalpel from the table, and slit his loose, unshaven, foreign neck from ear to ear. The scalpel was sharp. The cut was clean. The death was quick. I thought that was a shame in some ways. I did for Mrs Garcia by shoving her head in the autoclave. That was a far messier job, what with the boiling water splashing everywhere and the fact that her head was too big to fit, but with perseverance I finished the job.

I then turned to the three goldfish bowls on the table. All three heads looked at me and began babbling, but the head that had been Terry's, and was perhaps, in some sense, still Terry's, babbled loudest of all.

'You two shut up,' I said to the other heads. 'I want to hear Terry beg and plead.'

'Eric,' he said, 'am I glad to see you!'

'I can't think why.'

'I know I took your job and made you look like a criminal, but you know, that's all in the past, isn't it?'

'The very recent past,' I said.

'But a lot of water's flowed under the bridge since then.'

'True, Terry. Very true.'

'I mean, at least I went to the trouble of coming out here and telling you how I'd stitched you up. I didn't have to do that you know. In fact, if I hadn't come here and told you, then I'd never have run into the Garcias and they wouldn't have cut off my head.'

'Life's ironical like that, don't you find, Terry?'

'Look Eric, I know you don't owe me anything . . .'

'Too bloody true.'

'And I know I don't deserve much, but you can see me here, the state I'm in, the bloody misery of it all. I'm not asking much, but if you've got an ounce of forgiveness and humanity in you, then disconnect these wires that are keeping me alive. That's all I'm asking, Eric. Just kill me.'

I smiled at Terry. I patted his goldfish bowl, and walked out of the caravan. His screams, and indeed the screams of the two others, called after me, but they weren't very loud. They were muffled by the glass of the goldfish bowls.

Kathleen was waiting for me when I returned from the Garcias. She was trim and attractive as ever. She was hot. She was eager. She tore my clothes from me, and we rutted on the grass by the children's playground. We rolled over and over in the dewy grass as I brought Kathleen to shattering climax after shattering climax. When I'd done that fifteen or twenty times I stood up. I towered over Kathleen. She looked up at me worshipfully.

'You've been a good wife to me, Kathleen,' I said. 'But not good enough.'

I picked up the M-16. I felt the weight of it, the balance and elegance of design. It felt good. I pointed it at Kathleen. She looked at me without flinching. She didn't panic or plead. It would have been easy to pull the trigger and rid the world of one faithless wife, perhaps too easy.

'I've been true to you, Eric, in my fashion,' she said. 'Don't shoot me.'

I still couldn't deny that woman anything. I didn't shoot her.

It's after midnight now. The old journal's taken quite a bit of writing today. Kathleen is sleeping soundly. The Tralee

Carapark and Holiday Centre is the very epitome of peace and quiet. It seems like a great place to spend two weeks' holiday.

It's been a long and full day. I'm pretty whacked but very fulfilled. They say revenge is sweet, and they're not wrong.

Of course, I haven't had a *complete* revenge. There are a number of people who still haven't had what's coming to them, people like the booksellers of Skegness, the building workers who rode away with Kathleen in their van, the androgynous pair who stole our laundry, Hollerenshaw's police colleagues who twisted my arm and waved a truncheon in my face, the incompetents at the hospital, the previous occupants of this caravan, my so-called parents, my neighbour Ken, the people who burgled my house, the chap I ran into on my way here, my muggers, the person or persons who threw a brick through our window on our first night, the inventor of truth games, the owner of the site shop, whoever put a human finger in my meal, the people who thought it was a good idea to open a burger bar at the Tralee, whoever's responsible for all this freak weather, the younger generation as a whole, even Max and Sally, if we're really being honest.

But as I sit here now, peaceful and relaxed, feeling at one with it all, and at one with myself, I think I can afford to be generous and merciful. I've decided to feel sorry for them all.

Saturday

Woke up this morning, and oh my Lord, it had all been a dream.

The alarm-clock was bleeping. I was at home in my own bed, in my own house that hadn't burned down. Kathleen was beside me, and she hadn't turned into a lustful hellcat, and we would go down to breakfast together with our own dear children who hadn't discovered nature and religion and hadn't become lost to us. We weren't at the Tralee Carapark and Holiday Centre, the holiday hadn't been unremitting torture, and I hadn't slaughtered all the inhabitants of the site. In fact we'd never gone on holiday at all. The whole thing had been a nightmare, but a *real* nightmare, the sort you only get in your sleep, possibly brought on by eating too much of Kathleen's peach and pigeon sauté the previous evening.

I awoke to just an ordinary day. Ordinariness had never seemed so appealing. I sang 'These Foolish Things' as I went into the bathroom to run myself a nice hot bath. I checked the date on my watch. My forty-fifth birthday wasn't for a few days yet. Perhaps the dream had been a kind of premonition. The lads in the office had been trying to persuade me to go out boozing on my birthday. I'd never really liked the idea, but now I was absolutely certain that I wouldn't be going. I didn't want to risk looking at myself in the mirror of the Devonshire Arms and provoking a mid-life crisis. I'd been warned.

Then I really woke up, and oh my Lord, it hadn't all been a dream at all. The dream was to think it was just an ordinary day. I really was at the Tralee. The holiday really had been unremitting torture and I really had slaughtered all the inhabitants of the site, and a few more besides.

Ah well, no use crying over spilt milk.

Kathleen stirred beside me. She opened her eyes, looked at me adoringly and smiled. We had some more hanky-panky and while I may not have been the formidable sex-god of the last couple of days, there was some consolation in the fact that Kathleen didn't seem to be the unassuageable sex-goddess of the last couple of weeks either.

'How are you feeling?' Kathleen asked me when we'd finished.

'Fairly bitter-sweet,' I said. 'Yesterday was a good day for me. I got a lot of things off my chest, and I feel much better for it. And it seems to me that our marriage has never been better. But I do worry about the kids. Where did I go wrong?'

Right on cue there was a polite knock on the caravan door. I got out of bed, and opened the door to find Max standing before me, his head bowed, his posture stooped. I have to say he wasn't looking his best. His face and head were covered in stubble. His body was stained with mud, animal entrails and primitive decorations. His nails had grown into thick, dirty claws. His teeth were green, and his breath would have stopped a charging Amazon at fifty paces.

Sinbad was with him, and he was a changed dog. No longer the murderous animal of recent times, he was now as placid as a lapdog, and this time I sensed that it was real and permanent. I patted his head. He lay down and rolled over to present his belly for stroking.

'Hello Dad,' Max said.

'Hello son,' I said non-judgementally.

'Have you got a razor I can borrow?'

I was a bit surprised by the request but I was happy to oblige. I supplied Max with shampoo, soap, deodorant, after-shave, toothpaste, mouthwash, nail-clippers, loofah, pumice stone, as well as a razor. I didn't ask any questions. When he returned from the shower block he was spotless. He borrowed a sober tie, white shirt and slacks from me, and the transformation was complete. He was a credit to his old Dad.

'What happened to all the other holidaymakers?' he asked.

'They died.'

'But how?'

'Natural causes,' I said.

'Pah!' Max spat. 'I've had it with nature. I still don't reckon much to civilisation either, but at least with civilisation you get a roof over your head.

'And I've been giving some thought to my future. Earth sciences are all very well in their place, but I can't see myself studying them for three years. I want something more practical. I think I'd be much better off working in the bought ledger office of a major chain of furniture retailers.'

I knew there were at least two vacancies in my old office. Being my son might put Max at a bit of a disadvantage, but Max is a bright lad, there's no great family resemblance, and so long as he changes his name, he must be in with a good chance of being taken on.

'That would be a dream come true,' Max said. 'You know, I feel I've made a right prick of myself this last fortnight, but at least I've learned something.'

'That's what life's all about,' I said.

'In fact, I've learned a hell of a lot, I really have. You remember what I said about wanting to kill you and sleep with Mum?'

I did, all too clearly.

'Well, I think I've grown out of it.'

'Good for you, Max.'

'And the attempted human sacrifice: sorry about that.'

'You're a good 'un, son. A real chip off the old block.'

We had a fairly emotional scene then. There was a lot of shaking of hands and slapping of backs, and Kathleen joined in and there was kissing and hugging, and I'm not ashamed to say that a tear or two was shed.

'This is what a family should be like,' Kathleen said.

'Yes, but it's not complete, is it?' I said.

We thought of Sally and were suddenly sad. Oh yes, I'd revenged myself on the Hell's Angels, but that didn't bring Sally back. Suddenly we heard the sound of an approaching motorcycle, and as it came into view we saw that the rider was none other than my own flesh and blood, my lovely daughter

Sally. Her thighs were clenched around the big beast, a serene smile on her unhelmeted face. She brought the bike to a halt beside us. She dismounted.

'Long time no see,' Max said casually.

'Blessed are they that have not seen, and yet have believed,' Sally retorted.

Still the same old Sally. Some things don't change. She looked around the camp, at the dead and occasionally mutilated bodies.

'Never mind,' she said. 'At least they've gone to a better place.'

I hope she was right.

'Oh incidentally,' she continued, 'I'm pregnant.'

I've always thought I gave my kids a fairly decent sex education. I admit I felt a bit awkward when it came to describing the mechanical details, but I made sure there were always a few helpful, educational pamphlets and old biology text-books lying around at the appropriate times. And if I haven't been able to stop them squandering the precious gift of sexuality, at least I thought I'd drummed into them to be careful and not have an unwanted child.

'Who's the father?' I demanded. 'If it was one of those Hell's Angels . . .'

'Of course not,' she said. 'Though you might say that angels had something to do with it.'

I didn't understand that remark. I couldn't think who else but the bikers it could have been. She didn't have any boyfriends back home, in fact I'd never seen her so much as look at a boy. It vaguely crossed my mind that Max might be the culprit. It seemed like just the sort of thing he might do if he was in one of his bolshy moods, but I couldn't really see Sally going along with him.

'You can tell me,' Kathleen said.

'I will,' Sally replied. 'I intend to tell the whole world.'

'Well?'

'I know it's very difficult for people to believe in virgin birth these days . . .'

She didn't need to say anything else. I didn't argue with her.

Nobody did. There didn't seem much point. Those Hell's Angels had a lot to answer for, fortunately they'd already answered. They'd obviously turned Sally's head. They'd made her lose her reason. We were very gentle with her, very patient, and I resolved that I'll get her some of the finest psychiatric help that's available. It's the least a father can do.

'If it's a boy I'm going to call it Eric,' she said.

'Very nice dear.'

'You know,' Kathleen said, giving voice to feelings that I think we all shared, 'we haven't necessarily had things all our own way on this holiday. There have been a few raised voices, a few lost tempers, but now that we're all together like this, I think this is the best holiday we've ever had. I could stay here forever.'

This didn't seem like the time to ruin everybody's day by telling them that our house had burned down, so I didn't. Instead, I said there was absolutely no reason why we couldn't stay on at the Tralee for another week, two weeks if we felt like it. The family thought I was being a bit wild and irresponsible, and acting out of character, but they seemed to admire me for it, and they readily agreed. The rest of the day flew by in a glow of happy holidaymaking.

It's after midnight now. We've spent a quiet family evening in and around the caravan. I noticed yesterday, as I was running through the young chap with the stutter, that he owned a portable colour television. He won't be needing it now, so I went over to his caravan and took it. By and large I think it's shameful the way so many people spend every evening watching television and never speaking to each other, but this was a special night. There was a double-bill of Joan Crawford films being shown; *Forsaking All Others* and *Strait Jacket*. I was in seventh heaven.

Kathleen really excelled herself with supper. I fancied eating *al fresco*, and Kathleen came up with the splendid idea of barbecueing Sinbad. It was a stroke of genius. With a little black pepper and some English mustard he was a taste-sensation.

The family is asleep now. The Tralee is as quiet as the grave, but in the distance I can hear two-tone horns. I suppose it could be a fire or a road accident, but I suspect they're coming for me. In a way I hope they are. The sooner everything gets sorted out the better. I shan't be putting up a fight. I'll go quietly. 'Don't worry, officers,' I'll say, 'I can explain everything.' In fact I won't even need to do any explaining. All I'll have to do is show them this journal.

Epilogue

I'm afraid I don't actually know what day it is today. I've been here for quite a while now, and frankly the days are all much of a muchness, and I've rather lost track. I've also been fairly bad about keeping my journal up to date, but again, since all the days have been alike, I really wouldn't have had very much to report. But lately I've been putting one or two thoughts together, in order that posterity can have a full and frank account of my life and times, and I now feel ready to set them down. Here goes.

The best thing about being here is that I've been able to really have a break and a rest. I've been able to unwind completely. I've never felt so unwound. I'm absolutely relaxed, and that must be largely because I've been sleeping so well, better than I have for years. I get a good ten or twelve hours a night, and I always wake wonderfully refreshed. And the sleep isn't troubled by dreams, no more nightmares about vaginas with teeth or falling down bottomless pits.

And no doubt all of this is because I'm a lot less tense than I used to be. All the things that used to make me angry and irritable, all those daily trials and tribulations, they just don't get to me anymore. It's all water off a duck's back to me these days. Funny when you think about it, isn't it?

Accommodation is excellent. The room has everything you could possibly desire. It's compact but it probably gives you more room than you get when you're sharing a caravan with three other people. It's very clean, and the soundproofing is excellent. Very occasionally you may hear some distant screaming or laughter, but nothing you could possibly complain about.

The climate is excellent; a constant warm temperature, breezeless and air-conditioned. There's not much fresh air, but you can't have everything. The food's good. Of course it's not as good as Kathleen's home-cooking, how could it be? It's plain and simple, but plentiful, skilfully cooked, attractively presented, and completely free from foreign bodies. I could recommend it to anyone.

The staff are excellent. Their only concern seems to be to make my stay a pleasant one. They're not exactly overloaded with intellect, but I've never been a snob about that sort of thing. They ask me quiz questions, like what year it is, what my name is, who's the current Prime Minister. I think I get most of the answers right, and that seems to make them happy.

I haven't met many of the other residents. They keep themselves to themselves, and that suits me fine. I do miss not having Kathleen, Max and Sally around, but no doubt they're off somewhere having their own kind of break. At least this way I really do get away from it all.

I'm not saying it would suit everybody. A lot of people might find things a bit dull around here. I can't go for a constitutional, there's nobody to play beach-cricket with, not even Monopoly or Cluedo, and although there's a library of sorts, I can't say that I rate very highly any library that doesn't contain a coffee-table volume on Joan Crawford.

On the other hand, the lack of excitement is a small price to pay for the total absence of worries and aggravations. There's nobody playing music at all hours. There's nobody dropping litter. Nobody tries to con you, or mug you, or rape you, or threaten you, or humiliate you, or cuckold you. It's great. I can't remember when I last felt so carefree.

And my health has been first rate. I suppose that's because of the drugs. The drugs may also explain why I'm sleeping so well, and indeed why I'm feeling so carefree. But I don't care what the reason is, just so long as I don't have any worries.

There's no work to fret about, no responsibilities, no car, no house, no family, no insurance, no bills. It's just one long holiday. And the best part is, it isn't costing me a penny!

I asked them to get me some postcards so I could write to a few friends. They humoured me. They gave me the cards and a coloured pencil, and let me write postcards to my heart's content. I remember that we never sent any postcards all the time we were at the Tralee Carapark and Holiday Centre, so, since I've now got so much leisure, this is an opportunity not to be missed.

The postcards don't have pictures on them. They're just blank, which seems somehow very appropriate. I never know what to say on a postcard so I just settled for the usual, 'Wish you were here.'